PLAY ME

Brit Boys Sports Romance

J.H. CROIX

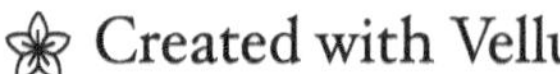 Created with Vellum

This one goes out to my mother who taught me what it means to be true to yourself.

Sign up for my newsletter for information on new releases & get a FREE copy of one of my books!

http://jhcroixauthor.com/subscribe/

Follow me!
jhcroix@jhcroix.com
https://amazon.com/author/jhcroix
https://www.bookbub.com/authors/j-h-croix
https://www.facebook.com/jhcroix
https://www.instagram.com/jhcroix/

Chapter One

TRISTAN

I rounded a corner, heading down the hallway to my office, and collided with a woman walking so fast, she nearly knocked me over. Her blonde hair flew in my face, and she caught her balance by grabbing onto my arm.

"Oh my God! I'm so... Ack!"

The woman exclaimed as her feet scrambled and, hell if I know how, she managed to drag us both to the floor in her tumble. It was then my body discovered that this woman was a veritable buffet of curves. I could feel her full breasts pressing against my chest and, as luck would have it, my cock was nestled at the apex of her luscious thighs. I still had no fucking clue who she was, but my body would've been happy to stay right where I was.

Small problem—she was wiggling out from under me inside of a second. "Oh my God! I can't believe that just happened."

Her voice sounded familiar, but I couldn't place it.

I had some manners, so I rolled to the side and pushed myself up. I glanced down to see her brushing her blonde hair away from her face and looking up at me. My heart nearly cracked a rib with its swift kick.

Daisy Knight sat on the hallway floor before me. Bloody hell, she was gorgeous. The last time I'd seen her had been almost a year ago. We had what I'd chalked up to an almost one-night stand I'd yet to forget. We hadn't even finished the act, and she'd left me more tied up than any woman—ever. I'd hoped to see her again and pick up where we left off. Yet, whether by accident or design, Daisy managed to avoid me so completely ever since then I figured that was her preference. Given that her two best friends were married to two of my best mates, I didn't doubt she'd gone out of her way to avoid seeing me. I had plenty of other things to focus on and eschewed attachments, so I'd figured I'd never get the chance to find out how amazing sex with her could have been.

Daisy's wide brown eyes met mine. Staring down at her with the feel of her body imprinted against mine, my cock twitched. Her lips parted—her plump lips with her slightly lopsided smile. I could see the rise and fall of her breasts with her breath. It didn't fucking help matters she was wearing a blouse that pulled tightly across them. My eyes dipped into the valley between them. My cock hardened, and I dragged my eyes up. Right. We were in the hallway in the medical research wing of the hospital. It wouldn't do to have me leering at her.

I held a hand out. "Hello, Daisy. Long time, no see," I said, keeping my tone level.

She gripped my hand, and I helped her up. Once she was standing, she brushed her hands over her skirt and adjusted her blouse. None of that made me forget a single inch of her delectable body. But I had manners and needed to respect the distance she seemed to want to keep from me. I took a step back.

"What brings you here?" I finally asked.

Her cheeks were slightly pink. Between the heavy fall of her blonde hair, those wide doe eyes, and her porcelain skin, the subtle flush nearly did me in.

She straightened her shoulders. "Hello Tristan. It has been a while, hasn't it?"

I nodded and considered whether it was worth mentioning the last time I saw her. Likely not, so I stayed quiet.

"Actually, I'm here to see Dr. Wells. He's temporarily covering the clinic for one of the studies I manage," she explained. "They told me his office was down here, but nothing's marked, so I lost track. What are you doing here?"

My heart gave another kick to my ribs. Daisy had known I'd graduated from medical school. She also had to know I'd been sidelined from playing ball last season after a brutal injury to my left knee. I'd spent most of my life playing football, otherwise known as soccer here in the United States. I'd signed with the Seattle Stars a few seasons back, along with several mates from England. All through university and through my professional career, I'd kept on track and finished my medical degree. It had been loads of work, but I'd known I wanted something other than sports for my career because it wouldn't last forever. I was lucky enough to be able to return to play soon with my knee finally back up to speed.

For now though, I was temporarily running the research clinic within the hospital while the director was traveling. A clinic that happened to have signed onto a study for a new medication trial before I took over. It was ideal for me because I didn't want a long-term position, just something to fill in for the next month or so. I should've connected the dots and realized they led straight back to Daisy, seeing as she was a lead medical researcher at the company the clinic had partnered with for the study. She appeared to have completely forgotten my last name.

I was about to answer when the flush on her cheeks deepened. "Tristan Wells. Right. I should've figured that one out. I bet you think I'm a dolt," she said with a wry laugh. "I didn't forget your name, it's just I've never called you Dr. Wells, so it didn't sink in."

"No one would ever accuse you of being a dolt," I replied. "Follow me."

I resumed walking toward my office, and she turned to follow beside me. I had a stern little convo with my cock on the walk down that hallway. Fortunately, it was a fair distance because my body's response to being near Daisy was off the charts. This woman just did it for me. She turned every invisible knob on the dials of my desire. I'd kept women in a tidy compartment in my life. I might have access to plenty, what with my college and then pro years as a soccer star, but I considered relationships messy. I had a healthy sex life, but it was more about enjoying the sex, and eschewing the emotional mess.

I stepped through my office door and gestured for Daisy to enter first. Her generous hips swayed with each step. As usual, she somehow managed to pull off this entirely professional way of dressing that had a hint of naughty to it. I knew how wild her response to me had been, so it only amped up my reaction to her. She wore a fitted skirt, a tad bit shorter and tighter than the usual professional skirt, that rested just above her knees paired with black kitten heeled shoes. Atop that she had on a fitted blouse. Perfectly respectable at a glance unless you happened to notice her breasts strained the buttons. She walked to the windows and looked out before spinning to face me. With her thick blonde hair, her heart shaped face and those brown doe eyes, bloody fucking hell, I wanted her.

I'd somehow managed to forget just how tempting she was. I reminded myself rather forcefully why Daisy was here. Work. Nothing more. Just because I wanted to bend her over my desk didn't mean it would be happening.

"So you're here to check in on the study protocol, I suppose?" I asked as I rounded my desk. Before sitting down, I gestured for her to take the seat across from me. Once she was seated, I sat down and leaned back.

She opened her purse and pulled out a pair of glasses. Fuck me. I'd never seen her in glasses. This would not bloody help. Oblivious to my internal state, she perched them on her nose and pulled out a small computer tablet. She tapped a few times and then glanced up.

"That's exactly why I'm here. When Dr. Horton signed the clinic on to our study, we were in the planning stages then. Since he left, there wasn't much to deal with, but now we're ready to start coordinating with you on patients who choose to enroll in the trial. This here," she paused and faced the tablet screen toward me. "...shows the process for how we'll track patients in our system. Since you've been here...?"

Her words trailed off with a questioning look.

"A few months," I added for her.

"Oh, then you must be familiar with this for the other study with our program."

"I am. It's very straightforward. The tech team here has already set up the online linkage for our unit, so there should be no issues."

Daisy closed the tablet and slipped it back into her rather voluminous purse before looking back to me. "Excellent."

A moment of silence fell, the air instantly feeling electric. What the hell was it with how she affected me? I'd better get a handle on it because as far as I knew I'd be working with her regularly now.

She drummed her fingertips on the arm of her chair and eyed me as if she was considering something. "So, how are you?"

I shrugged. "I'm well. Yourself?"

She worried her bottom lip for a moment, sending a shot of lust straight through me again. "Same, same. I'd imagine this last year might've been hard since you were out with your knee injury."

Ah, so I hadn't fallen off the face of the earth in her mind. "It wasn't great as far as that went, but I'll be back in play soon. Meanwhile, I'm here."

She kept drumming her fingertips. "I hope you didn't think I was avoiding you," she said abruptly.

If I'd been wondering, now I knew for

certain. Daisy was many things, but she wasn't one to shy away from something. Unless it bothered her.

For a beat, I considered politely going along with her. But I didn't quite feel like it. Rather, I wanted to push her.

I stood, my chair rolling back behind me, the sound of its wheels loud in the quiet office. Rounding the desk, I leaned my hips against it and looked down at her.

"I think you were."

Her gorgeous brown eyes widened, and she stood quickly. Oh bloody perfect. I'd pissed her off. Precisely what I wanted.

She was mere inches from me. I couldn't have planned it better. She rested her hands on her hips and glared at me. "I was not!"

I curled my hands on the edge of the desk, solely because if I didn't, I'd be yanking her to me inside of a second and that wouldn't do. Daisy and I had nearly set each other on fire with a few kisses and heavy petting. For reasons unknown to me, she'd put the brakes on hard and literally bolted away from me. Yet, I wanted to draw this out for the sake of seeing where it went.

I met her flashing eyes and arched a brow. "Really? You mean to tell me that in almost a year, you somehow managed to avoid every single time I happened to be with my mates? I find that nearly impossible. I used to see you every few weeks. We were about to let things go somewhere, and I haven't seen you since. What I want to know is why you're so tied up about it? Weren't you the one who said it was nothing?"

I was taunting her and I damn well knew it. Distantly, I wondered if I'd gone mad, but I didn't quite care to contemplate that just now.

Her cheeks flushed a deep pink, and she pointed at me. "I am *not* tied up about it."

Then, she actually jabbed me in the chest with her finger.

Chapter Two

DAISY

I knew I was flustered, and I knew I needed to get a grip, but I couldn't think straight. I jabbed Tristan's chest with my index finger and repeated myself. I hated when people repeated themselves, and here I was doing exactly that.

"I am *not* tied up about it."

Tristan looked down at me for a beat. Sweet hell. He was too handsome for words. He was tall, dark and mysterious, and so sexy it was dangerous. At least for my health and well-being. His black curls were slightly rumpled. His hazel eyes locked with mine, and my breath lodged in my throat. Heat spread like wildfire in my veins.

This was not supposed to be happening. About a year ago, I'd had a few too many glasses of wine, and I'd given in to the thrumming need Tristan had elicited inside of me ever since I'd known him. I'd meant for it to be nothing more than sex. I'd figured Tristan would let me down like every guy did. Problem was, once his mouth was on mine and his hands were mapping my body, I came closer to two things I'd been chasing forever—an orgasm and intimacy. Completely clothed with his mouth driving me mad and sweet streaks of pleasure shooting through me, I'd felt as if we were caught in a web together. I was so accustomed to sex being distant and mechanical—and completely unsatisfying.

With every fiber of me desperately wanting to let go into the best feeling ever, I'd shoved him away from me and bolted. Because all of it scared me. I knew perfectly well how Tristan viewed relationships. According to my two best friends who happened to be respectively paired up with his buddies from the Seattle Stars, he didn't do them. He declared them messy and steered clear. I'd always wondered why. Normally, I didn't mind being nosy, but I hadn't been able to bring myself to pry on this issue, too worried it would reveal just how personal my curiosity was.

So there I was nearly gaga over a guy who I just couldn't expect anything from. Little did he know I wanted nothing more than to settle down. I couldn't make a fool of myself over him. Leave it to me to be stuck pining for a man I couldn't have.

Tristan arched a brow. Hell, he even had an amazing face. Strong features with a blade of a nose, and a permanent five o'clock shadow. I remembered just how his stubble felt against my skin. As these thoughts tumbled through my mind, my pulse took off at a dash and I could hardly breathe.

He curled his hand around mine where my finger pressed into his chest. My belly did a slow flip and everything in me tightened with need. He was quiet, his eyes boring into mine. I felt prickly hot all over, exposed and vulnerable. On the heels of this came anger. It infuriated me that I wanted him so much.

"I think you are," he said, his low voice sending a hot shiver down my spine. "What I want to know is why?"

My cheeks were hot, and I willed the heat away, an entirely futile endeavor. I wanted to shake my head wildly and argue with him, but I didn't. My ability to speak deserted me the second he lifted his hand and traced it along my hairline, slowly sliding his fingers through my hair.

My breath came in short pants, while my pulse lunged. Need throbbed at my core. I wanted him so much. This was precisely why I'd avoided him. I knew how it felt to have him touch me, and it was so good, it pushed me past the bounds of sanity and made me forget everything else.

"If you're not lying, then have dinner with me," he said, his eyes never once breaking from mine.

Sheer stubbornness kept me from closing my eyes. I wanted to, but dammit, he was not going to see how much he rattled me.

"Fine. Let's have dinner," I snapped.

He still had my hand caught in his, while he idly sifted through my hair with his other hand. Heat rolled through me and my low belly clenched, but I would not let myself push him away. I could handle this. I'd show him he didn't have the upper hand, and I'd get over my body's obsession with him.

His mouth curled at one corner. Oh hell. God, he was too much for any woman to deal with and not lose her mind. "Tonight then?" he asked.

I didn't want to do this tonight. I needed

time to armor myself. But if I said no, I'd look like I was chickening out. I couldn't do that because, dammit, I had too much pride. He'd called me out on avoiding him, and I had to show him that wasn't the case. Never mind that I had *totally* been avoiding him. So I nodded and willed myself not to moan at the feel of his fingers brushing against the skin of my neck as they slid through my hair.

When I nodded, his eyes widened slightly. Good. He'd expected me to put him off. Hell no. I could handle this. It would be good. I needed to get past the awkwardness I felt and stop avoiding him.

He released my hand. I stepped back, maybe more quickly than I should have, but I needed to get some distance between us. His eyes took on a gleam and instantly I knew he'd noticed. I lifted my chin. "Where and when?" I asked, my tone coming out bitchy. I didn't care. I needed my inner bitch loud and proud right now.

"I'll pick you up. Six o'clock."

I so didn't want him to pick me up, but if I argued about that, it would seem silly.

"Fine. Don't be cheap," I said as I turned to spin away.

His low chuckle followed me to the door.

I was about to step through it when he spoke.

"Daisy?"

I glanced back to him.

"We *will* finish what we started before."

My cheeks flamed hot again, but I clung to my dignity with my fingertips. "You don't call the shots," I retorted.

He shrugged. "Maybe not, but I know you want it as much as I do."

I had no words for that. He had no idea how right he was.

Chapter Three

TRISTAN

Brilliant. I'd just gone and set myself up for a few hours of torture. What the hell was I thinking? If there was one thing I didn't do, it was chase after women. I'd done that once upon a time when I was young and naïve. I'd learned quite thoroughly it wasn't worth it. Yet, it definitely felt like I might be awful close to chasing Daisy. I couldn't resist though. No more than a few minutes of hot, wild kisses with her, and too much felt unfinished. Then, there was her and the way she got under my skin. When she went all prickly, that did it. I was determined to push her past the walls she'd put up. A distant warning bell rang in my mind, but I was feeling downright stubborn about this. I didn't intend for tonight to end with dinner. I needed to finally get her out of my system and then we'd both be better off for it.

My desk phone rang, jolting me out of my mental daze. Only then did I become aware enough to realize my cock was still hard. Bloody hell. That's how much of an effect Daisy had on me.

I let the call go to voice mail and forced myself through a set of twenty pushups— right there in my office in my lab coat. The exertion was enough to take the edge off my raging hard on and get my mind focused again.

Hours later, I snagged my keys off the table by the door to my flat and walked outside. Inside of a minute, I was driving toward Daisy's flat. I knew where she lived because I'd been there a number of times before she began conveniently avoiding me. She had hosted a few gatherings there for our mutual friends and lived close enough I could've walked, but I intended to make this an actual date, so I was taking her to dinner across town. I knew she loved new places and had heard from a friend at the hospital that there was a great new Asian fusion restaurant.

I rolled to a stop in front of the duplex where she lived. The door swung open as I lifted my hand to knock. My eyes collided with hers and my breath seized for a moment. Fuck me. She was so beautiful. Her thick mane of blonde hair hung in loose waves around her shoulders. She'd changed from her proper, professional outfit into a white cotton shirt that was cinched at the neck by a bow just above her generous breasts. This was paired with a bright blue skirt that hugged her hips and swung playfully at her knees. She wore the same black kitten heels. I don't think I'd ever seen her wear makeup and tonight was no exception. Her rosy cheeks were enough on their own, while her wide brown eyes had thick lashes that curled against her cheeks. She wasn't a typical beauty. She had a slightly crooked mouth paired with a nose that tipped up. With her angled eyes, she had a tilted look to her. Altogether, she seemed impish. She was curvier than the average woman, but didn't make any effort to hide it. It took every bit of restraint I had not to kiss her just then, but I didn't.

I don't know how, but I knew I had to tread lightly, or she'd do just as she had before. Don't ask me why I didn't just forget about it. I didn't know why Daisy bolted on me last time, but I *needed* to see this through to fruition with her, so I could stop thinking about her. I didn't even like to consider how many times I'd jacked off to the recollection of what it had felt like to kiss her. It had been like stepping into fire—so hot and so fucking good I'd craved it ever since.

"Cat got your tongue?" Daisy asked, her tone acerbic and sly.

I'd been all but slack-jawed staring at her, so she had me there. I rallied and shrugged. "You look beautiful. Shall we?"

Her eyes narrowed slightly, and she lifted her chin. "Of course," she said briskly before stepping through the door and locking it quickly behind her. Her scent drifted up to me—a hint of honey and fruit. I forced myself to step back as she turned to walk down the walkway.

Opening the car door for her got me an eye roll and a huff. Daisy like this was like gas on a fire for me. I had to talk my cock down as I rounded the car and climbed in.

"So where are we going?" she asked once I pulled away from the curb.

"New place I heard about across town."

"And that would be called?"

I glanced to her as I rolled to a stop at an intersection. "Actually, I can't remember, but I know where it is."

"You can't remember what it's called, but you know where it is?" she asked with a wide grin.

"Exactly. I remember numbers well. The address is four fifty-nine Hawthorne Drive. It's over by the airport. It's a new Asian fusion place. I know you love to try new places, and it just opened last weekend."

I navigated onto the road that would get us most quickly across town, a bit relieved driving gave me something to do. I'd underestimated the effect Daisy had on me. I couldn't say if it was because it had been so long since I'd spent much time with her, but bloody hell. She obliterated my ability to focus. I needed a few minutes to get a grip. I wasn't used to wanting someone this much.

"Oh! I heard about this place. It's supposed to be really good," she replied, bouncing in her seat a little.

You'd think I had some sense, but I'd also forgotten how it felt to be around Daisy. I'd known her a good three years now. She was this odd combination of sly and sarcastic mingled with a carefree joy that bubbled up occasionally. Aside from the fact I'd always felt a buzz of electricity between us, I also enjoyed being around her. She was quite bright and funny. She loved debating and was good-natured about it.

"Ah then. Do you know what it's called?" I asked in return.

Canting my eyes sideways, I caught her lopsided grin as she looked my way.

"Nope, but you're supposed to know."

"Is that so?"

"Yup. You're taking me to dinner, so you should know. I'll let it slide as long as it's as good as promised."

I chuckled. "Ah, so if it doesn't live up to the hype, I'm in the doghouse?"

I felt her grin this time as I kept my eyes on the road and had to bite back my own. This was too much fun, and that should've bothered me, but I didn't care. I had a goal, and I intended to see it through. Tonight would end with me buried deep inside of Daisy. For once and for all, I'd get her out of my system and then we could be friends again.

Chapter Four

DAISY

"Oh my God!" I reached to steady the bottle of wine wobbling in the middle of the table in between trying to catch my breath from laughing.

In the year or so I'd been finding one convenient excuse after another to avoid being around Tristan, I'd forgotten how funny he could be. By the way, avoiding him had taken an enormous amount of fancy footwork. Olivia and Harper were my two besties. They just so happened to be married to two of Tristan's teammates from the Seattle Stars—Liam and Alex. They weren't just Tristan's teammates, they'd all known each other back in Britain before signing with the Stars here. We spent a lot of time together, what with dinners, games and the occasional party. I'd put tons of energy into coming up with reasons why I wouldn't be around whenever I knew Tristan would.

The stupid kiss had made me crazy. Actually, it had been a bit more than a kiss. I'd accompanied Olivia to an out-of-town game once when Harper couldn't go. Dinner, copious amounts of wine, and Tristan simply existing in all of his hot glory had made me decide I could give in to what I'd wanted for as long as I'd known him. We'd been at it heavy in the stairwell at the hotel. So heavy, his knee was wedged between my thighs, the pressure against my clit driving me wild. Between that and how insanely good it had felt to have his mouth on mine and his thumb teasing a nipple, well I'd just about freaked out when he pulled back and our eyes locked. My heart had squeezed and my breath had lodged like a fist in my throat—because everything felt intense and deep and more than I'd ever imagined. And everything I'd chalked up to never being possible.

So I'd shimmied out from between the wall and his hard, hot body and bolted to my hotel room for a night by myself. I'd cursed myself for forgetting to bring my vibrator because I'd been that bad off, and my vibrator was the one and only thing that had ever brought me to climax.

I'd felt so vulnerable and stupid about it all that I'd done my best to never see Tristan. I'd also turned him into a stuffy jerk in my head. He tended to be quiet, so the opening to make him stuffy and uptight was there. I'd conveniently forgotten about his sly, understated humor and how much I enjoyed talking to him.

He was, of course, a sports star. Yet that barely touched the surface of him. He was fucking brilliant, which I loved. He'd somehow managed to finish medical school by fitting his classes in around his grueling schedule as a soccer player. He clearly had a passion for medicine and research. Another thing I loved about him—he wasn't intimidated by a smart woman. My brain was my best asset. I loved my job as a medical researcher and loved talking shop. Much as I hated to believe women didn't receive equal treatment in medicine, we didn't. Not even close. I was quite accustomed to being ignored in meetings and seeing the surprise on faces when people learned I was the lead researcher on multiple studies. Tristan wasn't like that. He treated me just as I'd expect him to treat a male colleague and would even admit if he was wrong about something.

Despite knowing all of this about him, I'd turned him into a stuffy jerk in the year I'd been avoiding him. Probably a smart thing to do because right now I had two problems. I wanted him so badly my panties were drenched and had been for at least an hour. And I liked him. I *really* liked him. He was everything I wanted in a guy. I'd been scouting high and low, far and wide for the man of my dreams for the last few years. All to no avail. I had no trouble scoring dates, but sex was something I'd come to dread and I'd begun to think I'd pinned my hopes too high in expecting to possibly find a guy who turned me on *and* who respected me.

The waiter stepped to the table, effectively snagging the wobbly bottle of wine and glancing between us with a grin. "Well, it looks like we're having fun. Are we thinking dessert?"

I swallowed the last of my laughter and glanced over at Tristan, promptly forgetting what had been so funny. The restaurant had been as sublime as the reviews indicated. I'd had a stir-fry, allegedly a fusion of Thai and American themes, or so the waiter said. I'd enjoyed my meal, but it's a miracle I noticed anything other than Tristan. He was far, far too distracting.

Tristan's black curls were rumpled as usual. His hazel eyes caught mine across the table, one dark brow arching up in question.

"Of course! I'm dying to know what fusion desserts you have," I announced.

The waiter ran down a list. When Tristan wouldn't choose, I settled on some kind of chocolate cayenne thing. Our waiter refilled my wine glass and left with the now empty bottle of wine. I was already tipsy. I didn't want to make a fool of myself, but I needed the liquid courage and the softening of my anxiety the wine afforded me.

Tristan took a swallow of his wine and eyed me. "So, tell me the truth—why have you been avoiding me all this time?"

His question hit me right in the solar plexus. Warmth spiraled outward and my belly executed a slow flip. Oh fuck it. I had nothing left to lose at this point.

"Because it seemed messy. Now that we've had dinner, I can handle it again," I said, hewing to vagueness and hoping that would be enough.

"Messy?"

Oh great. He wasn't going to let me off the hook. Well, whatever. I might as well blurt it all out. Then, he'd run for the hills and save me the bother of trying to keep avoiding him. I took a gulp of wine.

"Uh huh. Here's the thing, you don't do messy, so it seemed best we not let things go any further. Because I want two things—a commitment and an orgasm. The order doesn't really matter. Since I know you don't want a commitment, I figured it'd be better if we forgot how great that kiss was."

Chapter Five

TRISTAN

I snapped my mouth shut the moment I realized I was slack-jawed staring at Daisy for the second time tonight. There she sat across from me, the light glinting off her blonde hair, those wide brown eyes locked to me almost as if she was daring me, and her fucking luscious lips curled up at the corners. I gave myself a mental shake and tried to keep a rein on my body. Her little announcement was a hard spur to the need that had been galloping through me all evening. It also sent me skidding sideways in my mind.

"An orgasm and a commitment?" I asked.

I managed to keep my tone calm, but I felt as if she'd whacked me upside the head.

I'd spent all of this evening with one end goal in mind—to finish what we started and get her out of my system. The very word commitment had me taking several steps back. I wasn't an ass. It wasn't that I thought commitment was bad in concept. It was just I'd brushed up against it once, and it didn't go well.

I'd been young and at university and definitely foolish. I shan't say I had good sense then, as like most blokes, my cock didn't always take me in wise directions. To keep it brief, I was seeing a girl. Things ended in dramatic fashion when her ex decided to call me out for a fight. Come to find out, she'd mostly been using me to get back at him. I didn't enjoy—at all—being part of someone else's revenge. My pride took a hit, and I'd liked her enough that I fancied us in a serious relationship. It stung. Things got even messier when she got back together with him, he dumped her again, and she tried to drag me back in the middle. My cock thought it was a fine idea until reality struck, and the cynical truth became apparent. Yet again, I was nothing more than fodder for whatever long game she was playing with her ex.

I shan't say I was horribly brokenhearted, but more that the emotional shenanigans just didn't seem worth it when it came to relationships and anything resembling commitment. By the time my brain spoke louder than my other head, I'd had my fill of the drama and had hewed to a practical approach when it came to sex ever since then.

With my mind flashing warning signs, I stared at Daisy across the table, thinking I needed to just forget any idea of getting her out of my system.

Her cheeks flushed deeper and she lifted her chin slightly before nodding. "Yes, as I said, in no particular order."

Curiosity burned through me. I shouldn't have been this curious, but it was Daisy and I was nothing resembling sensible when it came to her, or so it seemed. "Are you telling me you've never had an orgasm?"

"Not with a man," she said, her tone haughty.

I could sense the underlying vulnerability it took for her to say any of this. Daisy wasn't one to back down though. She'd determined she wasn't going to hide, so she barreled right at it.

There wasn't much that could've made

me want her more, but this did. I hadn't the slightest doubt she'd have an orgasm with me, but knowing she'd never scaled that peak with another man was beyond tempting. That and her boldness. Fuck me. I needed to get a grip. She wasn't after just an orgasm. She wanted commitment, something I didn't even have on my radar. I did single quite well. I had friends, I had family, and I had sex. It all worked smoothly.

"If not in any particular order, does it matter if the orgasm and the commitment go together?"

My question just strolled out of my mouth on its own—without my permission. I scrambled inside, falling back to logic. Maybe I could compromise. I wanted her—so fiercely it burned. Perhaps there was an in between option.

Her chocolate brown gaze held mine for a beat before she shrugged. "Maybe. I'd like to say yes, but I'm so cynical about it, I've pretty much resigned myself to the fact it's not possible." She abruptly tore her eyes from mine and took a gulp of wine. "Okay, that's enough. I explained and now I won't be avoiding you anymore. Let's move on."

I knew we should move on because anything else was inviting disaster. Daisy had been entirely correct when she indicated things could get messy. They absolutely would if I followed the siren call of burning need for her. Apparently, I was bloody stupid because I shook my head.

"No, let's not move on. You need to have an orgasm. I can't fucking believe you've had to suffer through sex without one."

She rolled her eyes. "Oh God. Don't get all cocky with me. You're a doctor, you know plenty of women don't have orgasms during sex. Men are inclined to put their needs first. It's not like I suffered, more that it was like a chore. I'd rather not be bored and find someone to settle down with while I'm at it. I don't think that's too much to ask. And why are we still talking about this? Unless you're volunteering, this is a pointless discussion."

Did I forget to mention how stupid Daisy made me? What I did next was colossally stupid.

"Maybe I am." I drained the last of my wine and eyed her. Thank fucking God the table hid the fact my cock was rock hard.

Her eyes widened and her breath came out in a surprised puff. Her cheeks went cherry red, and I wanted her like crazy. In short order, I'd talked myself into the idea I could persuade Daisy to agree to this without the commitment part.

"You don't do relationships," she said slowly.

"Let's start with the orgasm."

I didn't let myself ponder the insanity I was stepping into. My body knew once with Daisy would never be enough. Messy didn't quite capture how it would play out if we had sex and she ended up wanting more. Despite my feeble attempts to be rational, my mouth was miles ahead of my mind.

"It's not like anyone can see into the future anyway. There's no way to agree in advance to commitment, but I can promise you an orgasm."

I took stock. I knew what I said to be factually true. There was no way anyone who was sane and honest would promise a commitment ahead of time. All I wanted was Daisy.

I wasn't usually cocky, but I knew what Daisy's response to me had been. It was mutual. We'd been on fire for each other. All I had to do was feed that fire. Commitment be damned.

I expected Daisy to tell me to fuck off, figuring that would put an end to my insanity and give me an easy out. She didn't. She an-

gled her head to the side, her gaze considering. That lopsided smile of hers slowly
unfurled. She might as well have kicked me in
the chest. My heart set to banging against my
ribs.

"You have a point. Maybe I've been going
about this all wrong. I'll take you up on your
offer. If anything because I think you're too
cocky and doubt you can deliver on your orgasm guarantee."

Her words threw another match into the
flames already flickering around us. Lust
bolted through me.

Our waiter arrived at that moment. I
never looked away from Daisy. "You can box
up that dessert. We'll be heading out now," I
said before handing him my credit card.

He spun away and returned quickly, setting the takeout box and the receipt on the
table. Daisy broke free from our electric
stare.

"Thank you so much. Everything was delicious. We'll definitely be back soon," she
said as I added a tip and all but shoved the
receipt in the waiter's hand.

Through the blur of need, I managed to
settle her jacket over her shoulders and curl
my hand around hers before all but dragging
her out of the restaurant. I considered taking

care of matters right there in the car, but forced myself to wait. If I were going to be bloody insane enough to do this with Daisy, I'd do it right. That meant being somewhere I could strip her bare and see every inch I'd only felt pressed against me before.

Chapter Six

DAISY

My body was nearly vibrating with need. The force of it was so powerful, it wouldn't have surprised me if I levitated above my car seat. The air inside Tristan's car felt alive—buzzing with the electricity crackling between us. The drive from the restaurant back to my house felt like forever. Intellectually, I knew it was maybe fifteen minutes at best. Yet, I wasn't sure I could make it without exploding or melting or tackling Tristan as he drove.

I actually tucked my hands under my thighs. That's how badly I wanted to touch him. I wanted to scoff at his confidence that he could bring me to orgasm and I'd managed to knock him down a little, but I didn't know what to do with the way I felt around him.

The chemistry between us was so hot, I wouldn't have been surprised if the tablecloth had caught on fire back at the restaurant.

You're being stupid. You know that, right? You know Tristan doesn't want a commitment, so what the hell are you doing?

He has a point. No one can guarantee a commitment. I'd like to see if I can have an orgasm with a guy. If it can happen with anyone, he's a good bet.

This was a variation on a debate I'd been having with myself ever since I'd kissed him last year. It felt urgent now because it was real. There was a third voice that rarely spoke up.

Maybe it's you. Maybe something's wrong with you and you just can't relax enough to let it happen.

I didn't like this voice. It was a quiet, anxious voice of doubt that had gotten marginally bolder over time. I'd been on a serious mission to find a man. I wanted the whole thing—great sex, love and happily-ever-after. While my friends seemed to stumble into it, I'd tried dates, friends with benefits, and more. By the way, friends with benefits are stupid when you can't have an orgasm with anyone. In short, the more this voice of doubt tried to make itself heard, the more depressed I got about the whole thing.

Between my body being on fire and my

mind volleying debate points, I blessedly lost track of time and breathed a silent sigh of relief when Tristan turned onto my street and rolled to a stop in front of the duplex where I lived. I felt half crazy. I wanted him. So much. And yet I didn't want to be disappointed. Again. I was also terrified of the way I felt when I was near him and didn't know how to navigate any of this. I didn't know what was worse—amazing sex with him and then falling for him and getting let down, or letting this chance pass me by and never finding out what it felt like to have an orgasm with a man.

Before I had a chance to come to a conclusion—truth was, there was not much thinking going on, more of a muddled haze of desire I was picking my way through—Tristan was at my door, opening it. To top it all off, he just had to go and be a gentleman. He was ever polite and gracious. When I was feeling vulnerable, like now, it grated on me. It made me feel like he was together, while I was flailing inside and at the whim of my body's needs.

My annoyance—with myself and with his ever calm presence—propelled me out of the car in a huff. I brushed past him and walked briskly to the door. I lived in a duplex in a residential area of Seattle. It was a renovated bungalow with a wide covered porch and painted cheerily in white with bright red trim. It was early spring. The air was scented with flowers. With its rainy, damp weather, Seattle was a veritable plethora of bright flowers come spring. In a few weeks, I'd be busy planting my flowerboxes, but tonight that was the furthest thing from my mind.

I left Tristan to close the door behind us once we stepped inside and stalked across the room to flick on a lamp. My living room was rather endearing with a large bay window—cushioned reading seat included—to one side and a fireplace on the opposite wall. The room had an arched entry door and wider archway leading into the kitchen on the other side. I'd painted the walls a soft cream. The polished hardwood floors were softened with bright throw rugs and a sectional couch with luxurious pillows in the center of the room. I often entertained because it was a warm, inviting space. Just now, I looked around and it felt suddenly too intimate.

I gave myself a mental shake. I would *not* let myself get cowed by doubts. I'd accepted Tristan's challenge, and dammit, he was the one who had something to prove. Not me. I ignored the whispers, wondering if I was out of my ever-loving mind. I felt him approach —my God he was like a crazy hot magnet for me—and spun to face him. I stood beside the archway into the kitchen where I'd flicked on a single lamp. The light cast a warm glow. He stopped perhaps a foot away, his gaze locked to mine.

The air felt hot even though I knew it to be cool, cool enough to make me shiver, and heavy—weighted with all the time I'd spent avoiding him that had led to making me only want him more fiercely. Trepidation thundered with every beat of my heart, but I wasn't going to chicken out. Hell, all I'd ever had was boring sex, and I was a sport about it every time. I could handle this. I closed the distance between us and called upon the bold part of me. I placed my hand on his chest and dragged it down the center, stopping just shy of curling it over his cock.

I was heartened to feel the strong beat of his heart as I passed over it, and to see the ridge of his cock outlined against his jeans when I flicked my eyes down. At least I knew he wanted me. I lifted my eyes again. The second they collided with his, my breath caught and my pulse—already racing—lunged, and heat flashed through me.

"You have a point to prove," I said as I lifted my chin.

Tristan was quiet for a few beats, his eyes scanning my face and then dropping down. Hell, all he had to do was look and my nipples tightened as if begging for his attention. His eyes flicked back to mine.

"I suppose I do."

His gravelly voice sent a hot shiver over my skin, tightening my nipples even further and sending heat coiling low in my belly. He held still, so still all I could hear was the rushed beat of my heart. Anxiety started to unfurl. I could only handle this if I felt in control. That was the crux of what had sent me bolting away from Tristan before. My body spiraled out of control around him. I was so accustomed to nothing more than vague flutters of sensation that turned into disappointing encounters. I didn't like to contemplate what it meant that I wanted to wrest my control back because it made me worry I was the reason sex had turned into such a chore for me.

In a flash, thought fled when Tristan closed the distance between us. I reflexively stepped back, bumping against the wall behind me. The heat and strength of him surrounded me. I was torn between wanting to flee—to flee from how much I wanted him and how impossible it was to feel in control when he was near—and wanting to sink into him. Desire curled around us like smoke. He rested a palm against the wall and lifted the other to trail his fingers through my hair. I could barely breathe and my knees almost gave out.

I felt suspended in this hazy heat with desire rolling through me in waves while all he did was idly sift through my hair. My eyes greedily soaked him in. Sweet hell. He was too handsome for words. His dark rumpled hair, those hazel eyes and his chiseled features. It was a miracle I didn't melt to the floor right there. He had a mouth made for sin—full, lush lips. God, a man shouldn't have lips like that.

It had been quiet for too long, so my brain started to come back online. That was bad. I instantly started to worry that this good feeling wouldn't go any further, that once we got past this initial burst, it would lose its luster, and I'd feel like I was going through the motions again. I needed to not think because thinking led to anxiety and then I started to get restless and then...

"Daisy."

Tristan's voice snapped through the

churning in my mind. My eyes whipped up to his.

"Stop thinking."

His tone came out a bit too authoritative for me, like he thought he could just tell me what to do. In the heat of the moment, it didn't even cross my mind he'd proceeded to snap me right out of the anxious place in my thoughts.

I nudged his leg with my knee. "I can think all I want."

I felt snappy and flustered and didn't give a damn if I sounded precisely that.

His mouth curled at one corner. Oh God. That was dangerous. My channel throbbed with need. I swallowed and straightened my spine. This had the unintended effect of pressing my breasts into his chest. My nipples thought that was awesome.

"Of course you can think all you want. It's just now's not the time and place for it."

Before I could formulate a comeback, he dipped his head and fit his mouth over mine. That kiss from almost a year ago, the kiss I'd never been able to forget? We picked up right where we left off. Our lips collided and it was as if a flash fire engulfed us. The kiss wasn't gentle, it wasn't a tentative exploration, nothing you might expect from two people who'd hardly seen each other and shared only one hurried kiss. Rather, it was hot, wet, messy and wild. Inside of a second, he was devouring my mouth. His hand threaded into the hair at the nape of my neck, and his thumb stroked in a lazy pass over my pulse.

As fierce as our kiss was, he didn't lose control. He stepped closer, his knee sliding between my thighs. The subtlest pressure against my core, and need coiled tightly inside. My body was completely out of my control, and once again, I didn't know how to contain the wildness thrumming through me. Somewhere along the way, his lips were blazing a wet trail of fire down my neck while he palmed one of my breasts, his thumb stroking back and forth in maddening passes. My breasts were heavy and aching, and I was so restless and so needy, my hips were rolling against his thigh.

We were right back to where we'd been. The only difference was we weren't in the stairwell at a hotel, but we were here in my house. Lights flashed in the front windows from a passing car rounding the curve in the road. Awareness sliced through me, and I stiffened. Tristan lifted his head. Once again, the moment his eyes met mine, I felt raw and exposed, caught in a shimmering web of intimacy.

He was quiet, the intensity of his gaze searing into me. I started thinking. Again. That's all it took, and I couldn't relax. I started to say something, but he shook his head.

"We're not talking."

Once again, the clear authority in his tone rankled me. It snapped me back out of thinking and got me annoyed.

"If I want to talk, I..."

He kissed me again. It turned out kisses from Tristan were a rather effective way of shutting me up. His tongue tangled with mine before he drew back, catching my bottom lip in his teeth and tugging it lightly. He pressed into me, and I could feel every hard, hot inch of his cock cradled at the apex of my thighs.

"You know. I think I see the problem," he murmured, his lips brushing against mine.

"What?" I asked, my voice a ragged whisper.

"You're brilliant, which I love by the way."

A little buzz of joy flashed inside of me. It didn't hurt the least to have him actually notice the fact I had a brain, and I used it quite well thank you.

"Because you're brilliant, you think. A lot. Sometimes thinking isn't helpful."

Oh. I saw right where he was going. That little buzz fizzled, and I felt vulnerable, and I hated it.

"You're brilliant too," I muttered.

I felt the shrug of his shoulder. "I think too much sometimes too."

I knew he meant the comment to make me feel less defensive. It had the effect of that and also making me feel more vulnerable. Why did he have to go and be nice too?

"We're not having sex tonight," he murmured.

Excuse me. Oh, this would not do.

I leaned back and looked at him. "Oh yes we are. You guaranteed me an orgasm."

"Oh, you'll have an orgasm, but we're not having sex."

I knew perfectly well he was rock hard and ready, so I was confused. "Huh?"

Not the best example of my brilliance.

He stepped back slightly and slid his hands down my arms, pulling me away from the wall. "Trust me."

Chapter Seven

TRISTAN

I curled my hand around one of Daisy's and stepped toward the short hallway at the back corner of her living room. I'd just told Daisy to trust me, while I had no idea if I could trust myself. She had the craziest effect on me. Under normal circumstances, I'd have come to the conclusion that I needed to put the brakes on this encounter. Hell, I'd have never been so far off my rocker to suggest I'd give any woman an orgasm. Not for a second did I doubt that possibility with Daisy—the chemistry between us burned so hot and bright, it was blinding. It's a fucking miracle I hadn't come already, what with her riding my thigh and making those crazy breathy moans. I thanked the stars I had an iron grip on my control. Yet right about now, it wasn't enough because I should've started using my sense and walked away from this. I didn't. I couldn't.

It was obvious Daisy overthought sex. I could practically feel the wheels turning in her brain. She was one of the smartest people I knew. One thing you figured out when you focused on academics the way I had was the brightest people tended to try to think their way through everything. I supposed playing ball had saved me. My skills there had me wisely electing to go pro because I knew it would set me up financially in a way other options wouldn't. Hell, I loved playing ball, but my choice to go pro was purely practical. It was the way I lost myself in play that taught me how my intellect could get in the way. I was at my best on the pitch when I didn't think too hard and let instinct and skill run the show.

When Daisy was twined against me kissing me so fiercely, I thought I might go up in flames right there with her. She wasn't thinking then. The second she started to think, she got tense. When it came to sex, I loved it as much as any guy, maybe more. I didn't like it complicated, and I didn't like it tangled up with emotions. Yet, here I was letting Daisy step past me into her bedroom. Nothing could have stopped me, yet in the far reaches of my mind, I knew this was stupid and had epic disaster written all over it if I wasn't careful.

That's why I'd declared we weren't having sex. Maybe I was a masochist, but I had it in my head I'd lose too much of what little control I had if I gave into that tonight.

Daisy dropped my hand and flicked on a lamp by the bed. I took in the space. Her bed reminded me of her somehow—a poster bed with tall posts almost reaching the ceiling and a canopy of sheer white fabric draped atop it. She had a deep wine colored quilt with enough pillows to get lost in. The effect was the same bold femininity she carried. She walked back toward me, kicking her shoes off as she did.

I hoped she didn't notice it, but I swallowed and bit back a groan at the sight of her. At some point during the midst of our heated kiss, I'd untied the little bow between her breasts. My eyes were drawn to the valley between them, savoring the plump curves of them spilling above the loosened opening in her shirt. She put her hands on her hips.

"Enjoying the view?" she asked, her tone sharp.

I gave myself a shake. Control. I had it in hand. I could do this.

She stood to the side of her bed. In two strides, I was in front of her. I did exactly what my body demanded and threaded my hand in her hair and tugged her flush against me, fitting my mouth over hers again. If I could simply kiss her forever, I could stop thinking too. Here I'd been thinking she was thinking too much and I was mucking about in my own thoughts. I'd made her a promise, and I intended to keep it. I wasn't quite ready to admit I wanted to see her lose herself in pleasure as much as I wanted it for her.

She kissed like a fucking dream. Once our lips collided, she threw herself into it boldly. Just like she did everything. There wasn't even the slightest hesitation. Her tongue warred with mine, while her hands mapped my chest. I slid a palm down her spine to cup her luscious bottom—bloody hell, every inch of her felt amazing—soft, juicy curves that gave against me. I resisted the urge to grind into her hips because I didn't know if I could stay in control if I did that.

She moaned in my mouth, and blood shot straight to my hard cock. If I managed to keep my sanity, I should win a fucking award for it tonight. I lifted her against me, and growled against her skin when she wrapped her legs around me. Her skirt fell away and I could feel the damp heat of her core against me.

In a blur, I shoved her shirt off, almost tripping over it when I settled her on the bed. She definitely wasn't thinking anymore because she'd gone fucking wild and was swearing as she shoved my shirt up. I also wasn't thinking because I forgot I meant to make this all about her and stay in control. I readily assisted her and reached behind my neck to tug my shirt off. Somehow I hung onto my control and eased her down on the bed.

Much as I loved sex—and I *loved* sex—I found myself in a haze of need lashed with torment. I usually didn't have trouble maintaining control. I'd found it quite easy to manage distant friendships with benefits, mostly because I made sure no woman left my bed without being completely satisfied. They knew the deal—no strings and no expectations for anything even resembling casual dating. Being with Daisy was proving to test limits I hadn't known I had.

She wore this ridiculous excuse for a bra —this cream lace concoction that had her taut pink nipples playing peek-a-boo with me through the lace. With her blonde hair, she was fair skinned and every inch of it was flushed pink. She propped herself on her elbows and looked up at me and—I kid you not—licked her lips before rising up to hook a finger in a belt loop on my jeans. The fact I still had those on might be the only thing to save me.

She still wasn't thinking. In fact, she was flat out driving me insane. I couldn't recall ever wanting someone this desperately. When she dragged her hand up and down my cock, practically purring, I went into action. I had to wrest control back from her, so I snagged her hands in mine and stretched out over her, bringing them over her head.

She wiggled underneath me and huffed—actually huffed. I'd quickly learned kissing kept her quiet, so I dove right back into another mind-bending, scalding hot kiss. I only tore my lips free when she moaned in my mouth, and I didn't give myself a chance to pause. Bloody hell, she tasted good. I licked, kissed and nipped my way down her neck, only then easing my grip on her hands as I mapped my way down her body. Much as I wanted to dally and tease through the sheer lace, I needed to taste her more than I needed to breathe. With a flick of my thumb, her bra fell open and her full, lush breasts tumbled loose.

I dragged my tongue around a nipple before sucking it in, beating back the urge to grin when she moaned and gripped my hair. The wilder she got, the harder it was for me to stay in control, but I managed. I teased her nipples with my fingers and mouth. Only when she was rocking her hips restlessly did I move along, trailing kisses over her belly. She smelled so fucking good—this sweet honey smell with the subtlest hint of some kind of berry. Every time I wanted to dally, I forced myself to keep moving because Daisy wasn't thinking and it needed to stay that way.

I managed to convince myself I could handle this all through dragging my fingers over the wet silk between her thighs—her panties were as ridiculous as her bra, nothing more than a scrap of cream lace. I wasn't one to care what women wore, but fuck me, everything Daisy did was like a hot bolt of lust for me. She was so brainy and practical, this feminine streak of hers made my cock so hard, I was seriously wondering if I could get through tonight without burying myself inside of her.

I was hanging onto my control by my fingertips when I dragged her skirt off. She wasn't a passive participant and when I leaned back to drop her skirt on the floor, she shimmied out of her panties and stroked her hand over my cock. That would not do. My control was beyond frayed at this point. I didn't wait another second and slid my palms up her thighs and spread her knees. She looked like she might be about to say something, so I purposefully looked away, only to end up staring at her pussy.

It was drenched and quivering. Her folds were pink and swollen and moisture coated the insides of her thighs. Bloody fucking hell. I should be able take a dispassionate approach to this. I'd seen more than my fair share of pussies. I gulped in air and lightly dragged a finger through her folds. She was so ready. My entire purpose of this insane torture was about to come to fruition because at this point I'd have sold my soul to make Daisy come.

Whatever she meant to say got lost in a long, low moan. I might've been on the edge of my control but if there was one thing worth losing myself in, it was her pleasure. I sank a finger slowly inside of her, savoring the pulses of her channel around me. I meant to draw this out, to give her the best fucking orgasm she'd ever had, but she made that all but impossible.

With her hips rolling into my touch, I couldn't hold back and brought my mouth to her. She was salty and sweet with a tang, and the moment I started exploring her, she gripped my hair and ground into me. I forgot everything and just threw myself into this—licking, stroking and sucking until I sensed she was about there. Only then did I swirl my tongue around her clit and suck it into my mouth. She came in a noisy burst, my name raining down around me in the midst of her pants and cries.

I drew back and leaned on an elbow. She was glorious. Her blonde hair was a wild tangle on the bed. Her skin glistened with a sheen of sweat, and she was rosy all over. What I wanted to do was kick off my jeans and sink inside of her. I knew how good she felt—tight and wet—and I knew she'd throw herself into that as much as she had this. But I didn't know if I could handle it. So despite the fact, I had the hardest hard-on I'd had since I could recall, I dropped a few kisses on her belly and eased up beside her, snagging a few pillows to prop us up on.

After a few beats, she opened her eyes and rolled her head to the side to look at me.

One look, and my heart clenched. She looked raw, and it hit me right in the chest. She lifted her chin slightly.

"Fair enough," she said, her voice raspy.

"Pardon?"

"I didn't think you could keep your word. I stand corrected."

I had no fucking clue what to say to that, so I simply nodded. I didn't want to leave. In fact, I wanted to sink inside of her and then fall asleep with her lush body curled up against mine.

She leaned up on an elbow, rolling on her hip and eyed me. The raw look in her eyes faded, an impish look following. She dragged her hand over my cock.

"Are you sure about that no sex tonight thing?" she asked with a sly grin.

I wasn't sure about anything, but I could bluff.

"I am."

She bit her lip and shrugged. "That's silly."

It was actually. I wasn't ready to admit it was pure self-preservation at this point, so I shrugged in return.

"This was about you."

I meant that precisely, yet I hadn't expected the words to carry such portent. I'd taken her pleasure more personally than I'd ever taken any woman's pleasure. It wasn't simply about her, it was about me being here with her in the experience.

It's just an orgasm. That's it. A collection of nerve endings responding to stimulation.

Now she's had one with a man. You can move on now. Don't make it more than it is.

The second those thoughts passed through my mind, I leapt ahead. Now she needed to have an orgasm during actual intercourse. It was only fair. I still couldn't cross that boundary. I needed to armor up for that, or I feared I'd lose my ability to keep my emotions out of the equation.

Her wide brown eyes watched me, but she was quiet. After a beat, she grinned again and sat up, crossing her legs and leaning her elbows on her knees. She looked downright adorable.

"Well, I won't ever accuse you of being selfish," she announced.

No, not after this.

"I think I want that dessert."

She bounded up from the bed and snagged a robe from the back of the door before dashing down the hallway.

Chapter Eight

DAISY

I stood outside the entrance to the research wing at the hospital and gathered my nerve. I didn't even know if Tristan was here today. The last time I'd seen him was when he made a smooth exit from my place after he'd blown my mind a few nights ago. I'd been restless and jumpy, literally buzzing with a burst of energy after having the most amazing orgasm of my life. I kept replaying that entire night—everything from the fun we had over dinner to the way his hands and mouth felt on nearly every inch of my body. I have no idea why I'd leapt off the bed and gone to devour that crazy chocolate dessert we'd brought home from the restaurant. The dessert itself had been sublime. Yet, Tristan had used that opportunity to cover his gorgeous chest with his shirt and depart. I was still wondering if I'd missed a major opportunity all because I'd been too nervous and restless to sit still.

Seriously, my body had felt electrified with an overload of sensation. I'd also been nearly jubilant to discover I wasn't forever incapable of having an orgasm with a man. I supposed we hadn't had sex yet, but of late my last few attempts at having sex had made me want to cry from boredom. It had all gotten so mechanical, and I'd been downright depressed about it.

Anyway, my mind had gone full on haywire in the days since our dinner date. I knew I was overthinking, but I couldn't seem to stop it. Tristan had been teasing and friendly, but I'd felt a paper-thin wall coming up between us before he left. I still wondered why he'd insisted we *not* have sex. I knew perfectly well from his friends that he didn't shy away from it. I'd done a little casual reconnaissance in the following days to see what else I could sniff out about his current dating life.

Zoe Lawson was likely my best bet for information, seeing as she was engaged to Ethan Walsh who was Tristan's former roommate and best friend. Yet, I hadn't had a chance to see Zoe in the last few days. I'd had to make do with a few carefully tossed in questions when I had coffee with Olivia and Harper and gotten next to nothing more than what I already knew. Tristan played his cards close to his chest and only occasionally saw a few different women whom Olivia described as his 'appointments.'

"Because he doesn't do relationships. You just wait, when that man falls, it will be epic," she'd said with a laugh.

I'd had so many more questions, but I wasn't about to let on that anything happened between Tristan and me. That itself was making me crazy. I was an open person. Hell, I'd been blithely bouncing around trying to find the love of my life and telling the whole world about it. What I hadn't chosen to share with anyone was how disappointing it had all become. I'd watched Olivia fall in love, then Harper and once Ethan dragged Zoe into our world, it made me feel even more separate. I was so happy for all of them. I truly was. It was starting to feel like it hadn't been the brightest idea to tell the whole world what I wanted, so I'd gotten quiet about it lately.

Now this thing had happened with Tristan, and I needed to keep my brain in gear. Sex and nothing more. Maybe not even that. He'd proved his point. Maybe that's all I needed to know so I could experience that same yearning, burning chemistry with someone else.

Uh, right. Not even. That's once in a blue moon, lightning strikes kind of chemistry.

Yeah but...

But what? Move on. If you keep wanting Tristan, you're signing up for heartbreak.

Therein lay the problem. I wanted him so much. I wanted a chance for more. Because I liked him. I really liked him. Yet, I couldn't be stupid.

"Can I help you miss?"

A friendly female voice came from my side, and I turned to glance in its direction. An elderly woman was walking toward me. She was round all over with wide blue eyes, soft cheeks that I wanted to pinch, and a giant smile. She reached me and stopped. Her nametag said Mandy, Volunteer Navigator. She must've assumed I was lost. I supposed I was, seeing as I'd been standing there for God only knows how long. Actually, I knew how long once I glanced at my watch—almost ten minutes.

Me, who always hurried everywhere, was

standing in the middle of a hospital hallway staring aimlessly while I obsessed about Tristan Wells. God help me. I rallied a polite smile for Mandy, clutching my phone and wiggling my hand back and forth.

"Oh no. I was just checking my email. I know right where I'm going. Thank you."

Mandy smiled again and angled her head to the side, her perceptive eyes scanning my face. "Are you sure you're okay?"

Oh Jesus. Fuck a duck. I have no idea why, but it's what I said in my head whenever I was embarrassed. Obviously, I needed to keep that ridiculous thought to myself. Why, oh why did it have to be so easy to read me?

Get your shit together, Daisy. Fake it 'til you make it.

I dug deep and kicked all the muddled confusion to the curb in my brain. I'd be bold and stop worrying about any of this. I could rattle Tristan just as much as he'd rattled me. I smiled brightly at Mandy.

"I sure am okay, but thanks for checking."

Blessedly, the hospital pager system called for someone for the ER, and Mandy gave me a little wave and hurried off. I armored myself with an attitude and pushed through the doors to the research wing. Every step down that long hallway to Tristan's office, I conjured recollections of how annoying and stuffy he could be. By the time I reached his door, I was feeling plenty annoyed and not the least bit mortified about anything that had passed between us. I rapped sharply on his door and went in without waiting.

Tristan was standing with his back to the door. His hip was resting against his desk, and he was on the phone. He didn't appear to have heard me come in, so I closed the door quietly behind me. Good grief. Even his back was sexy. I could see the corded muscles through his shirt as he lifted a hand and ran it through his hair. Oh, and did I mention he had a great ass? When it came to men, that part of their anatomy could easily go unnoticed. Tristan was nothing but muscle everywhere, and his ass was tight. It hadn't helped me at all to see his bare chest the other night because I'd had plenty of fantasies about that and the rest of him bare and all over me since then.

I was so fucking screwed.

He kept talking to whoever was on the phone, and I thought perhaps I should leave. Even though I hadn't come in here for the purpose of eavesdropping, it didn't feel right to linger. I started to turn away when my ears perked up at the sound of a woman's name.

"Renee, no. I'm not up for it, and I'm definitely not going to explain. I never agreed to be at your beck and call."

Tristan's tone was firm and bordering on annoyed. If I'd been Renee, I'd have gotten pissed about it. He nodded along to whatever she said and then said goodbye before tossing his phone on his desk. "Fuck," he muttered, running his hand through his hair and turning toward the door.

I still had my hand curled on the doorknob and froze, feeling my cheeks heat instantly when his eyes met mine. We stared at each other for a few beats and then his eyes narrowed.

"Do you normally enter offices without knocking?" he asked.

"I knocked! I swear. When you didn't answer, I came in and then... Well, you were on the phone and I was just about to leave," I explained rapidly, annoyed as hell that this little moment knocked me out of the bold attitude I'd conjured up before walking in here. No matter any awkwardness between Tristan and I, I wasn't a rude person and would normally have turned right back around once I noticed he was on the phone. But I'd let my nosiness get the best of me.

He held my gaze for another beat and

then shrugged. "Okay." Another quiet moment passed and then he stepped toward the windows and rested his hips against the wide sill, curling his hands over its edge. His office had a great view of the Seattle skyline with the Space Needle off to one side and Puget Sound in the distance. "So what brings you by today?"

His tone was conversational and perfectly calm—absolutely no indication that he'd nearly melted me in my bed a few nights ago. Okay, I could play the same game. I'd act like nothing happened.

"I sent an email yesterday afternoon. We check weekly on screening data once patients start enrolling in one of our studies," I said pointedly.

"Ah, I'm sure you did. I haven't gotten through all of my email from the day before yet, so it's a guarantee I missed that one. Apologies. Shall we schedule a regular time then?"

He didn't even move from where he stood. His gaze held mine, polite and friendly. Nothing more. I started to get annoyed. Maybe I could play this game, but I wanted him to be as off kilter as I was.

I slipped my phone out of my purse and

pulled up my calendar. "Yes, let's do that. Shall we say Thursdays at three?"

When he didn't reply, I glanced up. He was still right where he'd been and had made no move to check his calendar. His hazel eyes locked with mine, and the air between us crackled to life. It was as if there was a line of electricity connecting us across the room. I ignored it, although my belly clenched and my core throbbed. I steeled myself. I would *not* be the first one to look away.

After an uncomfortably long moment, he nodded. "That works."

I sent a silent thanks to whatever angel was cutting me a break because I'd already entered the time in my calendar and could barely think enough to change it. I tapped save without looking and slipped my phone back into my purse before striding toward the small round table by the windows, never once breaking away from his gaze.

"So now works as well?" I asked as I stopped by the table, curling my hand on the back of a chair beside it.

"I suppose it will have to, won't it?" he countered with a gleam in his eyes.

I hoped he couldn't see how hard I was gripping that chair. As polite as his tone was, I sensed he was trying to get under my skin. No way in hell would I let on that he was succeeding. Honestly, I didn't know if it was him or me. It didn't matter. I'd have this meeting, and we'd discuss research data while I prayed the dryness of our topic would keep my panties from getting any wetter than they already were.

TRISTAN

I stayed right where I was and held onto the windowsill as if it would save me. Fuck. I was in serious trouble. Daisy showed up out of nowhere, and all I could think about was locking the door and finishing what we started the other night. She was so fucking gorgeous. Her blonde hair was up in some kind of twist today. All it made me want to do was take it down, so I could run my hands through her hair and kiss her until she was moaning in my mouth again.

She wore a navy blue fitted skirt that hugged her hips and flared at her knees. This was paired with a fitted white blouse and navy kitten heels. As usual, she looked perfectly professional, although her skirt was a tad flirty and the button between her breasts was pulled tight. Now that I knew she loved lacy lingerie, it didn't help me in the slightest to imagine what was behind that clean white fabric. Danger, danger. If I kept staring at her, I'd be rock hard all over again.

I'd left her place the other night with a raging hard on. I'd gotten home and headed straight for the shower where I'd jacked off to the memory of her pussy clenching around my fingers and the way she looked afterwards —flushed and pink and every inch of her so delectable it had probably been divine inter-vention that stopped me from burying myself inside of her. Thank fucking God she'd up and wrapped herself in a robe and started eating that dessert. Otherwise, there would've been no way I'd have managed to leave her side. As it was, it ranked as the one of the hardest things I'd ever done.

My mechanical release shortly thereafter had just barely taken the edge off of my lust for her. I'd woken the following morning with my cock rock hard again on the heels of an insanely hot dream about her. I honestly couldn't recall if I'd ever dreamt about a woman. If I had, I certainly didn't remember it. I was normally a rational man. Daisy made me the opposite. While the rational part of me was noting perhaps it was time to pump the brakes on my crazy idea to do anything with her, another part of me—a frankly foolish part of me—was downright reckless. I wanted Daisy like mad. Hell, I *needed* her. I'd do whatever it took to burn her out of my system. I was banking on that to help me return to sanity again.

I'd barely been able to keep her out of my mind the last few days and was bloody relieved I'd finally been cleared to start practicing with my team again. I needed the physical rigors of it to stay sane. I briefly wondered what Daisy had heard when she came in my office. Not much because I hadn't said much. Little did she know that entire conversation was her fault. Renee was one of a few women I occasionally saw. I'd seen her off and on for a year. Up until the day following my dinner date with Daisy, Renee had never put the slightest pressure on me. We saw each other every few weeks, maybe, unless she was seeing someone else. I wouldn't call what we did dating. Rather, we'd have dinner every so often and fuck. That was it. She'd called the other day, and I couldn't even fathom trying to fuck her, so I'd said I was busy.

It had never occurred to me before that I

didn't know how Renee would handle no because there'd been no reason for me to say it before. Well, she'd called three days straight since and was getting way too pushy about it. It was all Daisy's fault because now that I'd had a taste of her, I didn't want anyone else. I'd been running laps in my brain coming up with how to manage this issue. I'd loosely devised a plan, all based around the fact she'd had boring sex up until now. I'd make sure she had an orgasm in every possible way she wanted before we put an end to the madness. That should get her out of my system and would make up for everything she'd missed so far.

I wasn't cocky about sex, or so I didn't think. I just knew I wasn't selfish and went out of my way to make sure no woman walked away from an encounter with me unsatisfied. A distant voice murmured in the back of my brain—hell, it had been murmuring for days. Daisy's pleasure was something else for me. I had to witness it. It wasn't simply about making her feel good. I wanted it more than I wanted my own release, which was crazy and should've made me run as fast as I could away from her.

There was no way in hell I was doing that.

So I carefully eased my grip on the windowsill and stepped to her side. When my gaze flicked down to pull her chair out, I noticed her knuckles were white where her hand curled over the back of the chair. A thread of relief wove through me. Perhaps she was as bad off as me.

Her scent—honey and berries—wafted up to me, and I resisted the urge to drop a kiss at the soft spot where her neck met her shoulder. I pulled her chair out and gestured for her to sit.

"Need anything to drink?" I asked as she slipped into the chair.

My eyes, rather willful when it came to Daisy, couldn't help but flick down to notice her skirt rode up her thighs slightly.

"If you have water, that would be great."

Inside of two seconds, I'd forgotten I'd even asked her a question. Her reply snapped me out of fantasizing about her thighs wrapped around my hips.

"Of course. Let me get that for you."

I turned and strode quickly to the counter that ran the full length of the wall behind my desk. This wasn't technically my office, or my desk. It was Dr. Horton's, but he was gracious enough to allow me to use it for the four-month stint I'd signed up to cover as Director of Research while he was traveling. He conveniently kept a small fridge tucked under the counter. I snagged two bottles of water and returned to the table, sliding a bottle across to her as I sat down facing her.

"So what do you usually cover in these meetings?" I asked.

Daisy slid a computer tablet out of her purse and tapped the screen a few times before spinning it to face me on the table. "I like to make sure we're on track with what we see on our end. So far, it looks like Dr. Horton prescreened forty-five patients before he went on leave, and another thirty have been screened in since you took over. Even though our system links to the hospital's, I like to make sure what we see is consistent with what you have week to week. Beyond that, we like to check in weekly about any monitoring fluctuations, data points that form patterns, and of course all the usual issues such as patient response, symptom improvement, and side effects."

The next half hour passed rather easily. As I'd have guessed, Daisy was a pleasure to work with. She was inquisitive, bright and actually enjoyed diving into the data. By the time we finished, I'd managed to forget how ridiculously alluring she was.

She put the tablet away and looked back over at me. "Well, if we keep up like this, this will run very smoothly. Dr. Horton is wonderful, but you're a bit more organized than him," she said with a slight smile and a shrug.

"Ah, he does have a bit of an absent-minded quality, but he's one of the best doctors I've known."

"Of course. That's why I love working with him. Anyway, so that's what we do each week. Not so bad, right?"

I shook my head and idly spun the water bottle I'd almost drained in a slow circle on the table. Now that we weren't focused on research data, my body had tuned right back into Daisy's channel. I watched while she took a long slow sip of water. Bloody hell. With her lips wrapped around the end of the bottle and the soft skin of her neck exposed, my mind went two places at once—what it would feel like to have her lips wrapped around my cock and the vivid memory of the taste of her skin. She set the bottle down and swiped her tongue across her lower lip, catching a drop of water at the corner.

Lust bolted through me, hardening my cock inside of a second. I had a quick little convo with my cock, a rather weak attempt to talk it down. Normally, I'd be standing to walk her out about now. Or rather anyone else I might meet under these circumstances. If I stood, my arousal would be quite obvious, so I stayed right where I was, willing my body back to sanity.

Then she went and stood up, gathering her purse and hooking it over her shoulder. Her skirt caught on the arm of the chair, rising just high enough for me to see a glimpse of cream silk and the round curve of her delectable bottom. She appeared not to notice this and snagged her water bottle as she stepped away.

The chair tipped over, bumping her legs and leading her to stumble. "Oh My God, I didn't even..." she exclaimed as she caught her balance.

I was up and around the table in two quick strides, steadying her by the arm. Of course, I hadn't been thinking and when she looked up at me, I realized we were mere inches apart. Her eyes slammed into mine. For a beat, we just stared at each other. The sound of her breath hitching reminded me quite forcefully that I was plenty hot and hard for her.

We stood locked in place with my hand

curled around her upper arm. After a taut moment, she looked away, her cheeks flushing pink.

"It seems like I have a habit of stumbling whenever I'm here," she said with a slight laugh.

For a second I was confused and then I recalled she'd dragged us both to the floor when I'd encountered her in the hallway last week.

"I suppose so."

I forced myself to let go of her arm and stepped past her to lift the chair her skirt had unintentionally knocked over. Only Daisy would have a skirt—a flimsy, flirty thing—that could take down a chair.

I carefully, perhaps too carefully set the chair upright and slid it into place by the table before turning back to her. She hadn't moved, so we were still too close. Awkward wasn't something I usually felt with women. I didn't even know if what I felt just now could be described as awkward. The problem was I wanted Daisy so fiercely, I didn't know what to do with it. I didn't want her to misread anything between us, yet even I wasn't so sure it was purely casual. I liked to keep the sex in my life in a tidy corner. I treated it almost the same as I did everything else—

something to fit in and enjoy for the time I gave it. Nothing complicated.

Certainly not this insane burning need for a woman I knew wanted much more than sex. My brain and body were at war with each other over Daisy, so much so I found the only recourse was to ignore the conflict. At the moment, there seemed no resolution for it. Unless I walked away now.

I flat out decided to ignore any rumblings in my conscience about what the future might hold. I wanted Daisy, and I knew she wanted me. Hell, the chemistry between us was enough to set the room afire. With a firm grip on my control, I eyed her.

"Shall we have dinner again?" I asked.

Damn. My mouth wasn't usually a few steps ahead of my brain.

Daisy's wide brown eyes held mine for a beat. It was an act of will to keep my eyes from drifting down to her breasts. For a flash, I wasn't sure what her answer would be. Then she nodded.

"Let's. When and where?"

"Tonight and wherever you want."

Her slightly lopsided smile stretched across her face. "Okay. I'll have to think about the where part. What time?"

Her answer put me back on firm footing

inside. Just knowing I'd have another night with her elicited an odd sense of relief. "I'll pick you up at six."

She nodded and turned away, striding to the door. I followed and caught her by the hand just as she reached it. I was acting purely on instinct, and tugged her to me, sliding my palm down the curve of her spine to cup her bottom. I almost groaned at the lush give of it. Her eyes widened slightly, and I knew she could feel every inch of my cock cradled at the apex of her thighs.

I didn't wait and fit my mouth over hers. She didn't hesitate, opening her mouth and sighing into our kiss. I had to force myself to keep it brief, a few strokes against her tongue and then I pulled back.

"Tonight. Six o'clock."

She nodded and spun away, quickly exiting my office. I leaned against the door jam and enjoyed every swing of her hips as she walked down the hallway. I didn't stop watching until she turned the corner.

Chapter Ten

DAISY

I swung my little compact car into a parking spot at my office and sat there. My channel was throbbing and I could feel the wetness between my thighs. I'd lost my freaking mind. I don't know how I survived that meeting with Tristan without climbing across the table and straddling him. He'd been all cool, calm and collected. So much so that I'd felt ridiculous over how much he affected me. I shouldn't have been thinking that way, but I was so relieved I'd almost fallen over and he'd gotten up to help me. The ridge of his cock had been completely visible, outlined as it was against his black slacks. He'd been dressed more formally than I was accustomed to seeing. I had to admit I liked it.

God, with his dark, rugged athleticism packaged in black slacks and a button down shirt, it made me want to rip his clothes off.

Maybe you should stop thinking about him. You have two more meetings this afternoon, and you can't be sitting here horny and wet.

Right. I needed to get a grip. I gulped the last of the icy water from the water bottle and hurried back into work. I spun through two more planning meetings and then rushed into my office to plow through emails before I left for the day. I was a lead medical researcher at the Seattle branch of a pharmaceutical company. I loved my job. All through medical school, I'd known I wanted to work in research. I loved data and I wanted to be involved on the front end of innovation. I'd lucked into a position with a company that actually had a stellar reputation in medical research, a hard thing to find when it came to pharmaceutical companies. We focused mostly on life saving medicine trials and vaccines.

I was just finishing up when there was a knock at my door. I called out for whomever it was to come in.

"Hey, hey," Bradley Connors said as soon as he stepped through the door.

I closed up my email and spun in my

chair to face him. Bradley leaned in the doorway with a grin. He was a friend and the guy I'd tried to do the friend's with benefits thing that turned out to be nothing more than a letdown. I'd thought it would be fun because Bradley was fun, charming and handsome with his perpetually rumpled brown curls, dark eyes and outdoorsy vibe. We'd never discussed it, but after a few 'dates' where we enjoyed the alleged benefits of our friendship, I'd personally decided I'd rather we just be friends without any benefits. I hadn't wanted to discuss it because it meant either telling him he bored me silly in bed, or pondering if something was wrong with me that I couldn't relax and have a little fun.

"Hey, how's it going?" I asked as I snagged a pen and flipped it between my fingers.

"Same, same. You?"

"Busy as ever."

"Was wondering if you wanted to grab dinner and drinks tonight?"

I looked over at him and could sense he was hoping there might be more to it than that. After we'd faded out of things before, he'd gotten hot and heavy with another woman at the company.

"No plans with Sara?" I countered.

Bradley shook his head with a slow smile. "Nah. She got the wrong idea."

"About what?" I asked, honestly curious.

"You know me, Daisy. I like to keep it light. She wants more."

Aha. So Bradley was hoping I'd return to my place, which I'd only occupied maybe a few times over a period of months. Right now, the entire idea felt distasteful. It was nothing more than a convenience for Bradley. I didn't think he was a jerk, or even that he was trying to use anyone. He was just looking for someone who fit the bill.

My mind flashed to the way it had felt to be with Tristan the other night. Nothing more than a brief thought and my belly clenched. The idea of even attempting any-thing with Bradley now was impossible. Tristan would probably ruin me for anyone. I should've been worried about this, and I was. Just not enough to talk myself out of seeing what else I might experience with him.

I eyed Bradley. "You're always honest. Gotta give you that," I said with a chuckle.

He flashed a grin that I thought he meant to be charming. "So?"

"I've got other plans tonight. Speaking of that, you can plan on keeping me in the friends with no benefits category."

He arched a brow and shrugged. "Fair enough. You seeing someone then?"

Bradley was simply that straightforward. He was a decent guy and would probably be quite happy for me if I told him I was. I wanted to say yes, but I didn't know what to call what I was doing with Tristan, so I shrugged.

"Sort of. Things are early, so keep it quiet, okay?"

He sobered, his eyes coasting over my face. "You're an amazing woman, Daisy. Any guy would be lucky to have you. If I were looking for something more, you'd have to chase me away," he said, his tone completely serious.

I was surprised. I don't know what I expected, but it wasn't this. "Thanks. I think?"

"I'm dead serious. You rock, so make sure if this guy's good that he treats you right. If not, I'll set him straight."

At that, he gave a wave and left. My office door clicked shut behind him, and I sat there wondering just what to think. Was it that obvious I was hoping for something with Tristan?

Um, you're gaga over him, so probably.

I was so screwed. A part of me, a very big part of me, worried I was setting myself up big time with Tristan. Yet, even if he broke my heart, which was a pretty certain thing if what I knew about him was accurate, I didn't want to miss out on what might be the best sex of my life. He'd already given me the best orgasm of my life.

———

"So tell me when you'll be able to play again?" I asked, looking across the table at Tristan.

We were seated at a booth in another new restaurant—this one a bustling Greek diner named Apollo. There were statues and paintings of the Greek god scattered about the place. It had a tacky feel to it, what with the salt and pepper shakers shaped like Apollo, but the food was as delicious as the local papers had declared. I took a sip of wine and eyed him.

Tristan looked so good, I wanted to lick him all over. As was always the case, his black curls were a tad rumpled. He wore nothing other than a navy blue t-shirt, which served to show off his perfect chest, and worn jeans that hugged his muscled legs like a lover. I'd decided tonight he had the best forearms ever.

Forearms. I was horny over forearms. God help me.

"I finally got cleared to practice last week, so I'll be playing when the season starts," he replied before taking a drag off his beer.

I watched, practically transfixed at the sight of him swallowing and remembering the wicked magic his mouth had wrought on me the other night.

Focus, Daisy. Focus. It's your turn to say something now.

"So Tim cleared you then?"

I was referring to Tim Maxwell, the physical therapist who worked with most of the athletes that passed through surgery with one of my besties, Olivia Reed. She was an orthopedic surgeon badass. Once she did the surgery, she handed them over to Tim who bossed them around all the way through their recovery. Tim was also a good friend of ours.

Tristan set his beer down, and his lips quirked. "Yes, Tim cleared me. He didn't make it easy, but he finally gave me the all clear last week. I'll still be working with him for the next few months. Coach wants me to baby my knee, and he figures Tim won't let me be stupid."

"More like Tim won't hesitate to call you out if you try to ignore him."

Tristan rolled his eyes. "Eh, no he won't. I tease him about it, but I trust that guy with my knee more than anyone. Hard to believe, but I feel stronger than I did before the ACL tear last season. Tim does not fuck about with recovery."

"Well, he works with the best surgeon around, so I'd say not."

I was super proud of Olivia and didn't miss a chance to say so.

Tristan caught my comment and grinned. "Of course, none of it would be possible without Olivia."

Conversation carried on, and I remembered yet again why I'd tried so damn hard to avoid Tristan. Aside from the fact he was drool-worthy by any standard, he was a great date. He was smart with that sly, understated humor. I enjoyed actually being able to talk work and have him not only follow along, but have something to contribute. To make matters even worse, while he could've easily gotten away with being cocky, he wasn't. Oh, he was confident, plenty confident, but not even a drop of that obnoxious cocky attitude so many guys waved around like they were waving their cock.

Did I mention yet I was screwed? As in totally, completely, one hundred percent screwed. In that vein, I intended to make sure Tristan lived up to the full intent of his promise to me last week. I'd wanted an orgasm with a guy, which he'd delivered. Yet, I wanted the full deal.

The moment my mind started heading in that direction, my body hummed restlessly. I knocked back the rest of my wine and stood quickly. I needed to move, or I'd be jumping Tristan right here.

"Let's check out the art gallery on the corner," I said.

We'd walked past a new art gallery that appeared to be having an opening celebration. I needed something to do other than obsess about getting naked with him, so I mentioned the first thing that came to mind.

Never one to be rushed, he finished off his beer and stood. "After you," he said, gesturing for me to walk ahead of him. I remembered my purse at the last second and hooked it over my shoulder. When we moved to make room for a waiter carrying a laden tray of plates, Tristan's hand rested on my low back and stayed there as we walked to the register. I was instantly disappointed when he removed it to pay.

Within moments, I was unaccountably delighted to have his palm like a hot brand on me again as we walked down the sidewalk. It was a cool evening, the air scented fresh from an earlier rain. We didn't talk as we walked toward the gallery, yet my mind was spinning its own little web of thoughts about just what the hell I was doing.

Shut up. You're doing what you're doing.

I knew it was bad when I was ordering myself to shut up. I was relieved when we reached the gallery and were surrounded with a bustle of people. Seattle was famous for a number of things, including its cluster of glassblowers. This new gallery was filled to the brim with spectacular pieces of blown glass—everything from small pieces to large installations. Translucent colors filled the space as we meandered through. The gallery was situated in a corner building that had once housed an old clothing factory. I'd have presumed the gallery would only occupy a small part of the building, yet it took up all of it. The glass artists worked on site, so we meandered through watching the artists at work and checking out room upon room of their artwork.

The gallery had gone all out for this opening with hors d'oeuvres served on small tables in every room and wait staff circulating with trays of wine and champagne. I was abuzz—inside and out—with the hum of my body's need for Tristan growing louder by the minute. His nearness made me crazy. It was fairly crowded, so we were often walking close with his hand hot on my back and me itching to have him slide it down over my bottom.

As I'd have expected, he was as engaging a companion here as anywhere. He chatted with a few of the glassblowers and kept pulling me into whatever he was looking at. All in all, I felt rather distracted and was probably drinking too much wine, but I needed something to take the edge off my restlessness. We exited what appeared to be the last room. I paused and glanced both ways in the long hallway. To our left was the way we'd come and led back to the main room. Looking to the right, I presumed we'd finally reached a part of the old factory they weren't using. A faded sign was atop the door —'Offices' was all it said.

Next thing I knew, Tristan slid his hand off my low back and curled it around mine, tugging me with him to the door. To my surprise, it opened when he turned the knob. In a flash, we were on the other side. He spun me around so quickly, my back slammed into the door.

"What..."

My question was cut off by his mouth slamming to mine. Oh, well, that was just fine. He crowded against me, and I moaned at the feel of him—every hard, muscled inch of him pressed flush to me. This was no slow, gentle kiss. The second our lips met, his tongue swept into my mouth. It was hot, wet, and rough. He tangled a hand in my hair, adjusting the angle of my head when he yanked his lips away and trailed them down my neck, muttering something.

Heat spread like wildfire through my veins, and I sucked in a breath. My channel throbbed with need, and I wanted him so badly, I ached with it.

I wore a blue silk blouse with a scoop neck that cinched at the top of my breasts with a ribbon. He caught the ribbon in his teeth and drew back, quite effectively untying it. The silk sagged, revealing my black lace bra.

"Jesus, Daisy. You're so fucking hot," he murmured, his lips making their way into the sensitive valley between my breasts.

I slid a hand into his hair—because I needed something to hold onto. "Tristan, what..."

My question ended on a moan when he

laved his tongue over my nipple drenching the lace. A shiver of pleasure ran down my spine. My nipples were so tight, they hurt.

"Yes?" he asked, belatedly enough I didn't even recall I'd said anything for a second.

I dragged my eyes open to find his waiting. My heart gave a hard thump when our gazes locked. I took a shuddering breath and scrambled for purchase in my mind.

"What are you doing?" I finally managed to ask, my voice raspy.

"I didn't think I could make it all the way back through this bloody place without kissing you," he replied bluntly.

I liked to consider myself a strong woman, one who didn't need the approval of a man to feel good about herself. Yet, hearing how much he wanted me nearly made me swoon, the effect heightened by the state of my body—liquid need burning like fire in my veins.

"Oh," was my brilliant reply.

His hand was palming one of my breasts. He chose that moment to drag his thumb back and forth over my nipple. I moaned because I couldn't help it. My sex clenched, and I could feel the slick, wet heat there. I needed more than just the feel of his cock pressed at the apex of my thighs. I needed him, all of him, inside of me.

"Should we maybe go somewhere?" I asked, for the first time glancing around us.

We were in a dingy hallway. This part of the factory didn't appear to have been touched in a few decades. The paint was peeling off a door to one side and the concrete flooring was covered in heavy dust. Dusty cobwebs adorned the corners.

When my eyes made their way back to Tristan, his mouth was curled at one corner. Oh fuck me. My channel throbbed.

"Perhaps we should," he finally replied.

He didn't move though. We stood there in the dingy hallway with the voices from the gallery filtering dimly through the door. His thumb kept teasing my nipple with idle strokes, and I thought maybe we shouldn't leave.

"I have an idea."

His gruff voice sent a shiver over my skin. Whatever his idea was, I didn't doubt for a second it was a good one. Hell, I'd have walked through fire at this point to have him inside of me.

"What's that?"

"You said you wanted two things, right?"

A dash of reality slapped at me. Yes, I

had. I wanted to have an orgasm and a commitment. I really, really didn't want to think about the whole commitment thing right now. Whatever. I wasn't going to play dumb and act like I hadn't said that. Although, how stupid I'd been? I'd thought the truth would be the guarantee Tristan would stay miles away from me.

"Right. You've partially met one," I replied, drawing on my bold self to taunt him a little. That's the only way I'd stay sane in this madness with him.

I could tell my dig hit its target. He arched a brow. "Partially?"

I shrugged. "Oh, I definitely had an orgasm, and you helped make it happen. But I meant an orgasm when I was having sex. You didn't deliver that."

Have you lost your fucking mind? You like him way too much and now you're pretty much daring him to take this to the next level.

I was out of my mind. No doubt about that. But I wanted what I wanted and I didn't want to let it pass me by. I figured I'd find a way to keep from falling any deeper into this emotionally.

His gaze darkened as we stared at each other. His thumb made another slow pass over my nipple and then he caught it between his fingers and gave it a pinch before stepping back. Without a word, he dragged my blouse back together and tied the bow. Only then did he speak.

"Give me a month. I'll make sure you have an orgasm any way you want. At the end of the month, we'll reassess."

"Reassess?"

I couldn't help the laugh that escaped. Leave it to him to sound so haughty and stuffy. That turned out to be a good thing, otherwise I might have started thinking. Rational thought would have reminded me I was setting myself up for almost certain heartbreak.

He held my gaze. "Yes. I figure you've got a few years of bloody boring sex to make up for. I'd like to take all the credit, but I'm no fool. I know chemistry when I feel it. We've got it in spades, so let's see if we can burn it off. Like I said before, you can't guarantee commitment in advance anyway."

He'd thrown the gauntlet down. Either I chickened out and walked away, or I took him up on his offer. Whether he knew it or not, he had my number. If he'd approached this any other way than the dare it felt like, I'd have told him to fuck off. Instead I found myself nodding.

He simply nodded in return and curled his hand around mine. In seconds, we were walking swiftly through the gallery. Tristan's height was an advantage. The crowd simply parted for him as he strode boldly through.

I practically had to run to keep up with him. All of the sudden, a thought stopped me in my tracks. I planted my feet. He swung back swiftly.

"Yes?"

"One condition," I said.

He merely arched a brow.

"For the month, it's just us."

I waited with my heart banging a staccato rhythm against my ribs. I was being reckless and stupid as it was. I wasn't up for wondering who else he was fucking while I was at it.

He didn't even hesitate and nodded. "Wouldn't have it any other way."

Chapter Eleven

TRISTAN

A soft drizzle started to fall as I drove back to Daisy's place. I forced myself to keep both hands on the steering wheel, although the sight of her bare thighs was an unholy temptation. Yet again, she was wearing a skirt that was just a tad too short for my sanity. I'd walked through that damn gallery, watching her hips swing and wondering what it would feel like to flip that skirt up and slide my hand between her thighs for over an hour. That's what had led me to shove through that door and kiss her.

I knew I was out of my mind with what I'd just proposed, but I didn't care. I was hanging my sanity on the hopes that a month of Daisy would burn out the chemistry be-

tween us. It was a long, taut drive to her duplex. By the time we arrived, I was beyond
caring about the fact I was still rock hard. I
forced my movements to stay measured as I
opened the passenger door and closed it behind her. My control slipped again as I
watched her skirt swing with every step on
the slate walkway to her door.

The door slammed behind us, and I spun
her back against it, fitting my mouth over
hers and pouring hours of need into hers. Her
purse fell to the floor, her keys following in a
clatter. Shoving her skirt up, I didn't even
bother trying to take it slow. I slid my hand
down her thigh, groaning at the feel of her
silky skin. Dinner and that fucking endless
walk through the gallery had been foreplay
enough to make me want to explode. I slid
my hand around her bottom and groaned
again when I discovered she was wearing a
thong.

God, I fucking loved how soft she was. I
couldn't resist squeezing the lush curve of her
bottom. I finally tore my mouth free when
she dragged her hand over my cock. Our eyes
locked, and I didn't even know how it was
physically possible, but my cock got even
harder.

I let my finger follow along the strip of

silk between her cheeks. The silk covering her core was wet. I dragged my finger roughly over it. "Fuck, Daisy. You're going to kill me."

She leaned her head against the door, those wide brown eyes pinned to me. Her mouth—fuck me that mouth—curled on one side in a lopsided grin as she stroked across my cock again.

"As long as you make good on your promise, I won't kill you," she murmured.

That did it. In a blur, I tore at her clothes. I needed to see all of her. I'd had enough of the taunting and teasing her body had done all night, hidden inside that silky blouse where I could see her nipples pressing against the silk and that skirt that shouldn't even be legal. At least, not when she was wearing it.

She didn't hold back and made quick work of my shirt before she yanked my jeans open and slid her hand inside my briefs. My cock jumped at her touch. I gritted my teeth and yanked on the reins of control slipping through my fingers. Much as I wanted this to be rough and wild, I wanted enough control I could make sure I didn't rush so much that I reneged on my promise to Daisy.

I stepped back.

Big mistake.

She stood before me, her skirt pooled around her ankles, her blouse and bra on the floor beside her. Her breasts—full and round with her nipples taut and perky, practically taunting me with their existence. Her hair had come loose from its twist and fell around her shoulders—a honey gold tousled mess.

If I touched her now, I didn't think I'd make it away from this door. I grabbed her hand. "Come on."

Thank fucking God she didn't hesitate, and thank fucking God her bedroom was only maybe twenty steps away. After nothing but a blur, we were on the bed, and I was stretched out beside her, devouring her skin with my lips and tongue. It would remain an utter mystery why Daisy had such shitty luck with men and sex before. She was the most responsive woman I'd ever been with. Just as she approached everything else, she went at sex with boldness. She was generally loud in conversation and just as much so in sex, except now it was breathy moans that nearly made me lose control, gasps and little cries. She swore plenty too, which I fucking loved.

"Fuck Tristan, stop that!" she exclaimed, trying to wiggle out from under me as I drew my tongue along the sensitive skin on the inside of her thigh.

I gripped her hips and looked up. My cock throbbed at the sight of her—her skin was flushed pink and her hair was a wild mess on the pillows.

"Why? It's obvious you like it," I countered, dragging a finger through her folds and savoring how wet she was for me.

Her hips rolled into my touch. After a low moan, she narrowed her eyes.

"Not fair. I want…"

I didn't wait for her answer and put my mouth right where I wanted it, sinking a finger knuckle deep inside of her right then.

Her head fell back. "Oh God."

I settled in, exploring every inch of her folds with my tongue while stretching and fucking her with my fingers. She came in a noisy burst, her hips bucking against my mouth.

She yanked at my hair. I was so close to the edge of my control, I couldn't draw it out any further. I'd had enough sense to snag a condom out of my pocket when I kicked my jeans off earlier. I smoothed it on and settled against her. The wet heat of her entrance kissed the head of my cock, but I waited.

I brushed her hair back. When her wide brown eyes opened and met mine, my heart gave a swift kick. For a flash, I didn't know what to make of how I felt, but my need for her drowned out everything else.

I laced my hands into hers. I meant to wait another moment, though it would be close to torture for me with every inch of her lush curves pressed against me and her legs curling around my hips. But Daisy was restless and bossy and didn't allow it.

She nipped at my neck and rolled her hips into mine, just enough the frayed thread of my control snapped. I surged into her in one swift stroke, sinking straight to the hilt. I'd only been imagining what it would feel like to be inside of her for days now. Her channel was hot, slick and clenching. I was accustomed to exercising some control when it came to sex.

With Daisy, the moment I sank inside her, I lost all control. With her rocking into me and her breathy pants and moans falling around us, I couldn't have held back if I tried.

Chapter Twelve

DAISY

I was awash in sensation—every nerve ending in my body sizzling with need and chasing after the most intense pleasure I'd ever experienced. It didn't matter Tristan had just sent me spinning into an orgasm with his wicked mouth and fingers. The moment he sank inside of me, his cock filling and stretching me, my body spun on its axis. Pressure gathered tightly inside, tiny pings of pleasure were still ricocheting from my first orgasm.

I wasn't thinking. At all. It was glorious. I felt the rake of his teeth on my neck, the slide of his cock in and out of my core where I was so wet, I could feel my own juices on my thighs where they hugged his hips. His stubble grazed my neck and sent shivers through me. Every sensation spun into the storm building inside. Finally, finally, he appeared to let go into the same madness galloping through me. His strokes weren't measured—they were hard and fast, his hips drumming into me. I needed it like this, rough, wild and unrestrained, because I couldn't hold back and didn't want to be tossed asunder in this sensation alone.

I could feel his body go taut as our skin slapped together. He released one of my hands and reached between us, his thumb expertly swirling in a hard circle over my clit. The tether snapped inside of me. Pleasure spun loose and rayed through me. I dimly heard my voice hoarsely crying his name with his own muffled shout of mine following.

I collapsed, dizzy from the force of my climax. He fell against me, immediately shifting his weight to the side. I didn't want him to draw away and reflexively curled toward him, keeping him deep inside of me.

His breath gusted against my shoulder, while mine came in shuddering, messy heaves. We lay tangled on my bed for several long moments until he slowly eased his grip on my hand and stroked his palm down the inside of my arm where it lay above my head.

The feel of his fingers trailing over that sensitive skin made me clench again.

With tiny ripples of pleasure radiating through me, my mind slowly came back online. Wow. I didn't have words for what had just happened.

I felt his fingers sifting through my hair and finally opened my eyes. I didn't know what I expected, but it wasn't the look I saw in his eyes. His hazel gaze was waiting for me, mere inches away in the pile of pillows on my bed. I didn't know how to interpret it, but my heart squeezed. He was quiet, his eyes coasting over my face. After a moment, he cleared his throat and started to move again.

My legs had a mind of their own and tightened around him. His mouth curled at one corner.

"Are we staying like this forever?" he asked, his sly, gruff tone sending a shiver up my spine.

Sweet hell. This was how bad I had it. I'd had actual sex for the first time in months. I'd had my first orgasm with an actual cock inside of me, and my body was so responsive to him, I could probably go another round right away.

My cheeks heated, and I forced my legs

to relax. "We don't have to," I managed, striving to keep my tone casual.

He didn't move though and kept sliding his fingers through my hair. I wondered what to say next. This was all rather new for me. It wasn't the sex per se. No, rather it was I'd gotten so used to disappointment when I had sex. I had it down how to extricate myself gracefully after a partner in question found their pleasure while I'd been bored out of my mind. Don't go thinking I had tons and tons of sex. I hadn't. I'd had two semi-serious relationships in college and med school and then I'd been trying for what felt like way too long to find the right guy.

Those awkward moments after being let down were something I was an expert at navigating. Sadly, I'd learned the hard way how oblivious most men were. To this day, I didn't think any guy I'd been with knew I hadn't had an orgasm. Anyway, back to now. What I didn't know how to handle was the awkwardness of having two amazing orgasms with a guy I could totally fall for, but who I knew I'd only have for a month.

Do NOT forget that. One month. That's it.

Right. I'd handle it.

I shimmied my hips back and was gratified to notice he reflexively started to keep me right there. Whether he noticed it or not, he stopped and eased back. I scrambled off the bed. "Shower," I announced before walking quickly into the bathroom off my bedroom.

I didn't even look back and was surprised to find Tristan stepping into the shower with me moments later. Steam cocooned us. I turned and lifted my face out of the water and almost choked at the sight of him.

It should've been illegal for him to be naked in front of anyone. Every inch of him was lean, honed muscle. He had a dusting of black hair on his chest that arrowed down. My eyes soaked him in. Meanwhile, he snagged the soap from my hands and set to sliding it all over me before soaping himself.

My heart gave another one of those echoing thumps, and I forced myself to remember our deal. A month. I'd get a month of him, and I'd enjoy every minute.

Chapter Thirteen

TRISTAN

"Good to have you back on the pitch, mate," Liam said, clapping me on the shoulder as he reached my side.

I caught a water bottle tossed my way as we walked by the bench on the way toward the locker room. I'd had a week of practice now and was so fucking relieved to be back on the field. Our season was starting soon. Meanwhile, I'd been cleared for practice and would be checking in with Tim twice weekly along the way.

I guzzled some water and glanced to Liam as we made our way down the stadium hallway. "Good to be back."

"How's the knee?" Liam asked as we rounded the corner into the locker room.

"Good, far as I can tell. Honestly, I feel stronger than I did before my surgery."

Liam flashed me a grin. "Of course you do. Olivia's the best."

My surgeon happened to be Liam's wife. He'd met her when he suffered his own knee injury a few seasons back. He was bloody gaga over her still. Daisy danced along the edge of my thoughts. I didn't want to wonder, but I couldn't help it. She was the first woman I'd even considered could keep me tethered. That's how much I wanted her. I mentally shook those thoughts away.

"I give Olivia full credit, mate," I replied with a chuckle.

Liam got distracted by someone else, so I moved to my locker, stripping down and heading for the shower. As I let the steaming water pour down over me, I idly flexed my knee. At this point, it was habit, testing to see if I experienced any pain of weakness. I felt nothing. I still sighed with relief every time. I hadn't forgotten the blinding shot of pain when I skidded and tore my ACL at the end of the season before last. I'd known right off the bat I'd be out for a full season. I was glad I'd had something else to focus on when Dr. Horton offered to let me manage the clinic while he traveled. My long-term plan had always been to focus on my medical career once I was too old to play pro anymore. Too old in the world of professional sports wasn't that old. Yet, I wasn't ready for it to end yet, so I was quite happy to bounce back as well as I had. Conveniently, Dr. Horton would be returning to take the reins over for the research clinic soon.

I soaped off quickly, my mind flashing to the other night with Daisy. I'd almost fucked her all over again when I followed her into the shower. Her skin flushed pink from the steam with soap bubbles sliding all over it had been enough to make my cock twitch only minutes after I'd spent myself inside of her.

That had been two nights ago, and I was already restless to see her again. I'd stupidly tossed out the idea of a month, not considering the fact that once the clock started ticking, I'd immediately begin worrying about the limits of the time I'd set. Fuck me.

Not much later, I was making my way outside when I heard Liam call my name. I waited by the doors until he reached me.

"You coming to dinner with us?" he asked.

"Didn't know we were meeting up," I countered.

My answer was a given because I couldn't

help but wonder if I'd see Daisy. We hadn't made plans after I left the other night, and I'd been wondering when I'd see her next. This whatever-the-hell-it-was thing with her wasn't anything of the usual for me. Usually, I hewed to carefully cultivated casual encounters. Renee had been a steady one for me until her little blow up. She'd texted me a few more times since then, and I'd sent her one last text, telling her to consider our arrangement completely over.

It niggled in the back of my mind that my interest in her and anyone else had dissolved into nothing. I knew the factor in that was Daisy and Daisy alone, and I didn't want to contemplate what that might mean. Nor did I want to contemplate the quickening of my pulse and the jolt of need that hit me just thinking about the chance to see her.

"Olivia says we are. I need a few mates because she's got Daisy and Harper with her," Liam replied, flashing a wry grin.

I chuckled. "Where are we headed?" I asked as we pushed through the doors into the chilly damp early evening.

"That Thai place," he replied.

"Alex coming?" I asked, referring to Alex Gordon, the Stars goalkeeper.

"Yup, he's probably already there. I'm

running late because Coach grabbed me to chat about the new guy. He wanted to know what I think. Whaddya think about 'im?"

We commenced walking toward the Thai place, one we frequented every so often. I considered Liam's question. He and I played offense with Liam the centerpiece as play-maker and me another central player as a center-forward striker. The Seattle Stars management did as most pro sports teams did in the off-season and made adjustments to the roster. We'd had a spotty year last season after my injury and another of our starters out with a back problem. That player chose to retire, so management had gone looking. The new guy was pretty good, but he was young and he was cocky.

"He's got the skills, but I'm not impressed with his attitude," I finally replied.

Liam glanced to me and nodded. "That about sums up what I think. Coach figures he's young and needs time to settle. He's here for the year, so I told him we'd try to train that attitude right out of him."

"Aye, we just might."

We reached the restaurant and entered. I was relieved to be out of the drizzle that had picked up on our short walk. Liam was al-ready halfway across the restaurant. I followed along and resisted the urge to pick up my stride when I saw Daisy sitting at the table.

She sat beside Olivia, the contrast in their coloring serving to highlight Daisy's bright, fair looks. Olivia had dark curls and green eyes. She stood to greet Liam, only to get swept into his arms for a kiss. By the time he set her down, she was laughing and blushing.

She looked past him to me. "Hey Tristan, how's your knee?"

I slipped into the empty chair beside Daisy. "Good as new according to Tim," I replied as Olivia and Liam sat down across from us.

Olivia flashed a small smile and nodded. "That's what he told me. You make sure to keep up your sessions with him as long as he recommends them."

"She loves ordering people around," Liam added with a sly grin.

Olivia swatted at his shoulder. "I'm just making sure he takes care of it."

"Where are Alex and Harper?" I asked.

"Oh, they begged off," Daisy commented from my side.

I'd been resisting the urge to look directly at her, mostly because I feared once I looked her way, I'd forget anyone else was here. I glanced to her, and a jolt of lust hit me instantly. Her hair was up in a twist, which only made me want to take it down. She looked as if she'd come straight here from work with a fitted blouse and skirt on. My eyes meandered down to see the bare skin of her thigh. Blood shot to my groin. I forced my eyes up, only to have them land on her lush mouth.

Fuck me. I'd have to get through this dinner with my sanity intact. I couldn't say why, but I didn't particularly want any of the mutual friends I shared with Daisy to know about what we were doing. A distant warning bell rang in the back of my mind, but I ignored it. I was relentlessly practical when it came to sex. This thing with Daisy wasn't practical by any means.

Another hard swat at those thoughts, and I focused on the moment. Dinners like this were so common amongst us, I should've thought nothing of it. Yet, this was the first one in roughly a year where Daisy and I both happened to be here. With the warm heat of her beside me, it was an ungodly temptation to slide my hand down her thigh. I consciously kept both hands on the table and looked over at Liam when he said something.

A waitress arrived and took our orders. Inside of a few minutes, conversation was carrying on as it should. I took a long drag on the beer I'd ordered, thinking perhaps a light buzz might knock down the need lashing at me.

"Oh, I can ask Bradley if you'd like," Daisy said with a laugh.

"Only if he's going to give me a deal," Liam replied with a grin.

Olivia nudged him in the side with her elbow, which she was forever doing. "Just because he's Daisy's friend doesn't mean you should get a deal."

"Why not, luv?" Liam asked with a chuckle. "It all depends on the friend. I thought you said he was a friend with benefits. One of those benefits should be getting me a deal on basketball tickets."

Olivia rolled her eyes. "Oh stop it. We can afford them, so don't be pushy."

Under normal circumstances, I wouldn't give a bloody damn about any friend of Daisy's, much less whatever Liam meant by *benefits*. Yet, just now, I had a rather powerful reaction to the idea.

I sensed a thread of unease from Daisy, but she brushed a loose lock of hair off of her cheek and shrugged. "I'll ask him and let you know."

That's all she said. I bit back the urge to

turn to her and ask just what the hell kind of friend Bradley was. That wouldn't do, not with Liam and Olivia looking on. I wondered what the hell was wrong with me. I didn't get jealous. Ever. Every woman I'd ever been involved with knew the deal. I did my thing, they did theirs. Anything that crossed lines ended the arrangement.

Yet, here I sat, wrestling against an entirely unfamiliar feeling. The only relief I felt came from the knowledge Bradley had failed to satisfy Daisy because every man before me held that dubious honor.

Chapter Fourteen

DAISY

I sat beside Tristan and wondered if I'd completely lost my mind. Well, it wasn't my mind per se. Rather, it was my traitorous body. With Tristan right here, I worried I might actually melt into my chair. Heat emanated from him, and it felt as if we were surrounded by our own force field—a humming electricity crackling with desire and need. Fortunately, Olivia and Liam appeared oblivious.

It was perfectly common for my afternoon to have gone the way it did. I'd met Olivia and Harper for coffee, something we did several times a week. The only problem today was I felt like I had a secret. Well, I knew I had a secret—namely what was going on with Tristan.

To make matters worse, somehow conversation landed on Tristan and his erstwhile reputation for treating sex as a convenience and nothing more. Harper, oddly enough, knew the woman who happened to be the other half of one of his arrangements.

"Oh my God, Tristan would lose it if he heard what Renee's been bitching about at the office," Harper had said.

Of course, my ears had perked up so hard, they might as well have physically swiveled in Harper's direction.

I'd tried to play casual. "What do you mean and who's Renee?"

I hadn't forgotten that Tristan had uttered the name Renee in the conversation I'd overheard in his office.

Harper just had to go and take a sip of coffee before answering, so I'd had to sit there with my heart pounding and anxiety tightening in my chest.

"She runs the HR department at our clinic. She's been bragging about how she sees him for months now. She had this idea she'd play it cool until he saw how amazing she was. Anyway, apparently he cut things off with her last week and now she won't stop bitching about how much he hurt her," Harper had said with a roll of her eyes.

It had taken most of my discipline to keep my mouth shut and not ask any more questions. When Olivia mentioned meeting for dinner tonight, I'd gone back and forth mentally over whether to go tonight, but I was so weary of making up excuses to avoid any event where Tristan might be. And I wanted to see him. Badly.

So here I was. At the last minute, Harper had begged off with a headache. Of course, Alex adored her and insisted on going home with her, so it left me at this dinner with two fewer people to distract me. Tristan's nearness had me wet, and I was all out of sorts because I couldn't stop thinking about Renee. Who I didn't even know. I was stupidly jealous of her even though it sounded like Tristan had stopped seeing her. Worse, I was rattled by what it all meant. I knew Tristan didn't do serious, yet here I was diving into a month of madness with a man who was guaranteed not to want to even consider something serious.

If it was just the sex, I could probably stay sane. The problem was I liked him. A lot. I was walking myself straight down the plank to heartbreak. Yet, even knowing that,

I wasn't turning down the month he offered. It was too tempting.

When Liam made his teasing comment about Bradley, I got a little uncomfortable. It's not like I had anything to hide. Hell, I'd been loud and proud about how I was scouting around for the right guy. I managed to keep my reply casual, but I sensed a thread of tension from Tristan. The bonus to that was it kind of pissed me off. He had no right to be tense about anything to do with whether or not Bradley was a friend with benefits.

I managed to reply casually to Liam and conversation moved on. I felt prickly and annoyed, which might be the only thing that kept me from doing something stupid.

I leaned back in my chair when our waitress arrived to clear our plates. When Olivia declined another glass of wine, I was slightly relieved. While the year I'd been avoiding Tristan had taken some gymnastics as far as my excuses went, tonight had been a new challenge. I didn't want it to be known I was Tristan's latest paramour. I knew Olivia would worry because she'd say he didn't want what I wanted.

As it was, I'd spent most of tonight's dinner trying to keep from ever looking in

Tristan's direction too long, lest my greedy eyes get locked onto him. I was flushed inside and out and relieved for the dim lighting. My last hurdle for the evening would be managing a graceful departure.

"Luv, you're tired and it's time to go," Liam announced, curling his arm over Olivia's shoulders and dropping a kiss on her hair.

My heart gave a little thump. I wanted a man who looked at me the way Liam looked at Olivia.

Do NOT go there. Your time will come. Don't you dare pin those hopes on Tristan. He's your ticket to one month of hot sex and nothing more.

If only my heart would listen.

Olivia smiled ruefully, catching my eyes across the table. "I am. I had an earlier than usual surgery schedule today, so I've been up since four."

"Exactly. Let's go," Liam said, standing and pulling Olivia up. "Mind taking care of our bill?" he asked, his eyes on Tristan. "I'll get the next one."

"Got it covered, mate," Tristan replied easily.

"Coffee in a few days," I said to Olivia with a small wave.

They made their way out of the restaurant, leaving Tristan and me alone at the table. I'd thought the last hour or so had been an exercise in restraint. The second we didn't have company, my body practically caught on fire.

I stood quickly. "Be right back," I said before I hurried away to the restroom.

I used the bathroom, not because I really had to but because I needed something to do. Afterwards, I stood at the sink and ran icy cold water over my wrists and splashed it on my face. I needed something, anything, to snap me out of the feverish heat rolling through me. I left the restroom, ordering myself to politely say goodnight and leave. When I didn't see Tristan, I felt a sense of relief followed immediately by anger. Wow. He didn't even have the manners to face me and say goodnight. Either that, or I mattered that little to him. Yet, this wasn't like him. He was unfailingly polite. Always.

Whatever. I grabbed my jacket and threw it on before threading my way through the tables and pushing out the door. Only to run right into someone.

"Oomph!"

I glanced up to discover the someone in question happened to be Tristan.

"I was trying to hold the door for you, but

you were walking so fast I didn't get to it in time," he said with a low chuckle.

The sound sent a shiver up my spine. God, I had it bad. All he had to do was laugh, and I wanted him.

The heat I'd managed to dissipate inside from the icy water rolled through me again. It was damp and rainy out, and I was hot all over.

"Oh, sorry. I thought you'd left," I said because I didn't know what else to say.

He let the door fall closed and stepped back. We stood under a small awning outside the restaurant. I tugged my rain jacket together in front, shivering slightly. I needed the chilly, damp air to cool me off inside.

I glanced up to see Tristan shaking his head slightly.

"What?"

"I have manners you know. I wasn't just going to sod off and leave you here without at least saying goodbye."

Ah. So he meant to say good night. That was probably for the best, yet I instantly felt peevish about it. I didn't stop to think and my next words tumbled out without a filter.

"Fine then. I suppose we can say we can handle dinner going forward. Let's leave it at that."

My tone was bitchy, and I didn't even care.

One dark brow rose in a slash, and his eyes narrowed. "Fine then? Oh that's rich, Daisy. How about you be straight with me and let me know you're still keeping your friends with benefits?" he asked, his tone sarcastic and dark.

I went from peevish to pissed.

Hands on hips, I glared at him. "I'm not keeping any friends with benefits," I countered with air quotes and a roll of the eyes. "Bradley's a friend from work and nothing more and hasn't been for months. You're one to talk anyway. You've got your little stable of women you keep. Who the hell is Renee anyway? Apparently, she thought there was more to what you had with her."

Tristan's eyes widened and then narrowed. His gaze went from annoyed to angry. He looked away, shaking his head slowly, before bringing his gaze back to me. "I don't have a stable of women, Daisy. That's fucking ridiculous. Since you're asking, I used to see Renee occasionally. I don't anymore. I have no idea where you heard what you heard, but it means nothing."

We stared at each other. I was still pissed he'd said anything about Bradley, but I was just as angry with myself. I didn't like how much it hurt to think about someone else Tristan might have been with. I shouldn't care about Renee, a woman I didn't even know. It wasn't just thinking about her that chewed me up inside, it was his quick clarification that it meant nothing. Once again, my words were skipping ahead of my brain.

"Is that what I am to you? Nothing?"

Oh shit. Not a good place to go.

He stared at me with the rain falling in a soft drizzle just beyond the edge of the awning and the lights of passing cars glittering on the wet pavement.

"What do you mean?"

"Nothing," I mumbled, looking away.

It was a near miss, but I could gloss right past this awkward little moment.

I spun back when I felt his hand curl over my arm. In a flash, he was inches away. I looked up, and my breath hitched at the intensity in his gaze. I didn't know how to interpret it, but it hit me hard, smack in the center of my chest.

"Nothing is about the opposite of what you mean to me."

His words were low and fierce. We stood there, staring at each other. I didn't know what to say to that, although my heart was thudding so hard, I feared he could hear it. The hope I kept trying to keep dormant unfurled like a flower inside. I swallowed against the wave of emotion cresting inside of me.

The door to the restaurant opened swiftly, bumping me right into Tristan. His arm slid around my waist, pulling me clear so the group of people walking out could pass by. Once they did and their voices faded as they walked down the street, he curled his hand into mine.

"Let's go."

There was no question I'd go anywhere with him in this moment, so I let him lead me to his car and drive me home.

Chapter Fifteen

TRISTAN

The sun filtering through the curtains woke me. I opened my eyes to see the clock by Daisy's bed read six in the morning. I rolled my head back toward Daisy and nearly groaned. Her hair was a honeyed tangle on the pillows. I was curled up behind her with her perfect, lush bottom nestled against my cock, which was waking up to this fact quite readily. Her skin was silky soft. I resisted the urge to stroke my palm down over the curve of her hip. Truth was, the only reason I didn't was I happened to be cupping one of her breasts. It filled my palm, the lush weight of it tempting.

My mind spun back to last night. I was fairly certain I'd gone bloody crazy, but I didn't care to ponder the potential problems associated with that just now. After I'd confronted Daisy about Bradley and she'd asked me about Renee, I hadn't been able to see past anything other than the need to have her. I'd been so fucking jealous of Bradley—a man I didn't even know. It should've been a relief to know they weren't still friends with benefits, but thinking about *any man* being with Daisy made me fucking insane. Then, she'd gone and asked me if she meant nothing to me.

Let's be clear. I hadn't meant to imply Renee meant nothing to me. No woman meant nothing to me. I'd meant whatever gossip Daisy had heard was nothing and not worth considering. Renee had been a friend with benefits in the truest sense of that description, save the after the fact understanding that it appeared Renee read more into the arrangement than I had. For that, I was sorry. But it didn't change the reality that ever since I'd gotten this second chance to see things through with Daisy, no other woman held the slightest interest for me.

As for Daisy, the idea she could even contemplate she might mean nothing to me was insane. She meant far too much, and hell if I knew what to do about it. I was highly attuned to the timeframe. I'd told her a month. A month had seemed like ample time. Yet, now it felt as if it could never be enough. It was starting to feel complicated. I couldn't even fathom how I'd back away from her at the end of this month.

Daisy shifted against me, burrowing closer and sighing in her sleep. At the feel of her bottom, my cock hardened, and I bit back a laugh. This was ridiculous. The effect she had on me made me question my control, something I'd never had to do. But then, she seemed to have the unique ability to push me past boundaries I'd never considered crossing. Exhibit A: I didn't spend the night with women. Too intimate, too many possible implications. Yet, here I was, waking up beside Daisy. It hadn't even crossed my mind last night that I should leave.

I hadn't even asked her if I could come in. I just had and then we'd all but set the sheets on fire before falling asleep together. I closed my eyes and figured my best bet was to go back to sleep. Daisy burrowed closer and made a soft sound. Fuck me. No sleep for me. Perhaps a cold shower would do the trick. It took all of my willpower to start to ease away from her. She felt so good—all warm, soft and sleepy. I managed to create perhaps an inch between us, only to have her roll over.

Bloody hell. If I thought the feel of her round bottom against me was a problem, her breasts pressing into me were even worse.

"Mmm, Tristan?"

Her sleepy murmur nearly had me rolling her over and sinking inside of her. God help me. I was in trouble. Serious trouble.

"Right here," I managed.

Daisy pushed up on an elbow, lifting her hand and brushing her tangled hair away from her face. Her wide brown eyes were unguarded in her just-awake state. Daisy unguarded was so rare, it hit me right in the chest. My heart clenched. She tended to come across as so strong, bold and sly. Seeing her like this did something to me.

She watched me quietly. Her hand slid through the ends of her hair and fell to my chest. I couldn't hide my arousal, so I didn't even bother to try. After a beat, her mouth curled at one corner in that lopsided smile of hers.

Without a word, she dipped her head and proceeded to drop hot kisses on my chest, shoving the sheets out of the way as she did.

If there was one thing I was accustomed to when it came to sex, it was control. Right now, Daisy upended that and ripped it right out of my hands.

I scrambled for something to hold onto inside.

"Daisy?" I managed to choke out on a rough gasp as she curled her palm around my cock.

She lifted her head, her hair a wild tangle of honey around her face. "Yes?"

"What are you doing?"

Probably the most inane question ever right about now. My body didn't want her to stop. At all. Yet, with control slipping through my fingers, I wasn't thinking too clearly.

She bit her lip and her eyes took on a wicked gleam.

"This," she said before leaning over and dragging her tongue along the underside of my cock.

I fell back into the pillows on a groan, giving myself over to her. She proceeded to drive me completely mad. I should've known she'd be thorough. She was a woman of attention and detail. Her tongue didn't miss a single centimeter—long, teasing strokes and swirls, damp kisses, the hot, wet suction of her mouth when she drew my cock inside.

I forgot about control, forgot everything

except the electric feel of her mouth on me and the pressure coiling so tightly inside. A slow drag of her tongue, her fist curled around me, and she drew me deep into her warm, wet mouth once more. Nothing but her name came with the roar of my release.

I dimly felt her lips making their way back up my chest and ending with a soft kiss against my neck before she curled up against me. I dragged my eyes open to find her grinning.

I was spent and managed a weak smile.

"Good morning," she offered brightly.

I couldn't help but chuckle. "A very good morning, I dare say," I managed as my breath slowed.

She dropped another kiss on my neck and pushed away from me, bouncing out of bed.

That would not do. With an effort, I pushed myself up and followed her, still reeling from spending myself in her mouth. I was moving slowly enough she was already in the shower when I caught up to her in the bathroom.

I climbed in behind her, and she spun around to toss another sly grin my way.

"What's so amusing?" I asked as she handed over the soap.

She stood under the water with soap bubbles sliding over her skin, still grinning.

"Oh, it's nice to catch you off guard. Plus, you've been spoiling me, so..."

Her words trailed off, and she flushed a deeper shade of pink. With the steam, she was already pink all over, which I loved by the way.

My cock promptly forgot it had already been taken care of this morning. I stepped to her. The soap slipped from my hands, falling to the tiled floor with a thump. I slid my hands up her hips and over her belly to cup her breasts. I grinned when her breath hitched. I didn't mind she'd turned the tables on me this morning, but I loved seeing her let go. I toyed with her nipples and followed the water down her skin. When she flexed against me and murmured my name, my control once again slipped through my fingers. I spun her around. She stumbled slightly and caught her balance on the wall. Perfect. Her lush round bottom tilted up at me. I reached between her thighs to find her hot, wet, and ready.

In a haze of need pounding through me, I positioned my cock at her entrance and was about to bury myself inside of her when reality hit me.

I stepped back so fast, I almost slipped on the wet tiles. She glanced over her shoulder.

"Where are you going?" she snapped.

"Condom," I choked out.

I had never, ever forgotten protection. That's how lost I was in the maelstrom of Daisy.

"Forget it. I'm totally clean and I'm on the pill. I know you're clean too because you guys are treated like royalty by your doctors. Just fuck me."

I stared back at her. In the far reaches of my mind, a voice tried to speak up, but I ignored it. Oh, I wasn't worried about protection per se. No, rather what it meant that I was about to get this close to Daisy. With any other woman, I wouldn't have even considered this. It was too intimate. I didn't care. All I knew was what I wanted.

I stepped back to her and slid a palm down her spine, savoring the arch as she flexed into my touch. I curled my hand around her hip, gripped my cock and slid into her creamy clench, sinking to the hilt at once. Her head fell forward on a low moan. Everything blurred, the feel of her sweet channel pulsing around me, the sound of her pants and moans, and the sensation roaring through me. All of it tightened until I felt her start to throb. I reached around and pressed against her clit, savoring the rough cry of my name. To be bare inside of her when she came was the most intense pleasure I'd ever experienced. My own release thundered through me. We stood under the pounding hot water with me curled over her.

After I managed to catch my breath, I regretfully drew out of her. I'd have died happy if I stayed right there buried deep inside of her. She straightened and slowly turned. I meant to say something, but I couldn't seem to speak. She lifted her hand and traced a single fingertip along my collarbone and down my arm before bending over to pick up the soap.

Later that day, I kept remembering the trail of that single touch. Every time I recalled it—hundreds of times—my heart clenched.

Chapter Sixteen

DAISY

The steady sound of my feet striking the treadmill soothed me. I ran in place for a solid hour before stepping off. It was raining today, so I'd headed to the gym rather than for a run in the park. I snagged my towel and water bottle and headed toward the showers. After a quick shower, I was almost dressed when I heard my name. I glanced up to see Zoe Lawson standing a few lockers away. She was in the midst of tying her shoes.

"Oh hey. I didn't even see you there," I said by way of greeting.

Zoe flashed a quick smile. "Me neither. Gyms are funny like that. I come in here so focused on minding my own business, I'm sure I miss seeing people all the time. How's it going?"

Zoe was engaged to Ethan Walsh, Tristan's former roommate and another British soccer player who'd signed with the Seattle Stars a few years ago. Zoe had become a friend over the last year. She was smart as a whip and beautiful with her rich auburn hair, hazel eyes and long legs. Along with many others, I'd been slightly amazed at how quickly Ethan had fallen for her. Ethan had once been a player for the ages. He'd never been an ass about it, but casual had been the name of his game. He'd met Zoe and never looked back. They were downright domestic now and had just purchased a lovely home in a residential area of Seattle.

"Pretty good, you?" I asked in return.

Zoe tied her other shoe and straightened as she began bundling her gym clothes into a bag. "Great. I'm busy as ever, but that's good."

We simultaneously slung our bags over our shoulders and glanced at each other. With a laugh, I gestured toward the doors. "Shall we?"

We chatted casually on the way down the hallway to the main entrance and paused once we were outside. Zoe glanced to me. "I was about to grab some coffee before I head to the office. Wanna join me?"

"Sure. Where to?"

"My fave is Desert Isle Coffee, but if..."

I was already nodding, so she paused and arched a brow.

"Oh that's my fave too. Let's go."

We walked the few blocks to Desert Isle Coffee and waited in line together. Once we were seated, Zoe took a slow sip of her coffee and eyed me.

"Mind if I ask you something?"

I instantly wondered what she might want to ask me, but I nodded.

"Are you seeing Tristan?"

I managed to keep my mouth from falling open, but just barely.

"Uh, no. Why do you ask?" I hedged, wondering how the hell she knew anything about Tristan and me.

"Oh, Ethan and I saw you two at dinner last week. He wanted to go over, but I told him not to because it looked like you were, well, like you were on an actual date," she explained.

I wished for about the thousandth time in my life that I didn't have such fair skin. I knew my cheeks were flushed and knew I couldn't do a damn thing to hide it. I considered trying to keep up the ruse, but it occurred to me Zoe might be a good person to talk with. Being engaged to Ethan gave her more up close and personal knowledge about Tristan than any of my friends, seeing as Ethan and Tristan were best buds.

I took a fortifying gulp of my dark coffee and set it down. "Okay, maybe we were. I'd rather it not be public knowledge if you don't mind though."

Zoe cocked her head to the side and nodded slowly. "Of course. Aside from you and the girls, who would I tell?"

"Well, that's the thing. Olivia and Harper don't know about it either."

Zoe's eyes widened. "Oh," was all she said.

I rolled my eyes and shoved at the uncertainty trying to push its way forward in my mind.

"Oh is right. I don't know what the hell we're doing. Here's the thing, about a year ago we had this crazy kiss. I know he doesn't want anything else, so I put a stop to it. It's no secret I'd like to settle down. Anyway, I ran into him through work because he's covering one of the research projects I supervise for the next month or two."

I paused because what could I say next? He kissed me and I melted? That made me sound like a swoony fan. I took another gulp of coffee and sighed. Meanwhile, Zoe waited patiently. I liked that about her. She didn't jump all over things, not like me.

"Ugh. It all sounds so embarrassing," I finally said with another sigh.

Zoe smiled softly. "Ah, well I can understand that. If I'd tried to explain anything that happened with Ethan and me when we first met, I'd still be mortified. Since you're not usually shy about talking about guys, I'm going to guess you like him. The way he was looking at you the other night told me all I need to know about how Tristan feels about you," she said with a low laugh.

She might as well have thrown food at me when I was starving. "What do you mean?" I asked quickly. Too quickly.

"Just that he was practically eating you up with his eyes." She paused and idly traced her finger in a circle around her coffee cup on the table. "Is there a reason this is all hush-hush?"

I nervously spun the silver bracelet on my wrist and considered her question. "No good reason, other than I'm worried I'm being beyond stupid. I don't really want to do the casual thing, and it's no secret Tristan doesn't want a relationship. It wouldn't even be happening if it weren't for the fact we seem to have a bit of chemistry. I didn't want it to be a thing with our friends, so I haven't said anything."

Zoe's gaze was thoughtful as she looked over at me. "I ruined it all because Ethan and I saw you two out. Well, here's what I think. Even before I saw you two the other night, I noticed Tristan pays quite a bit of attention to you. He might try to act like he can avoid a real relationship forever, but I doubt it. The way he was looking at you the other night, it's obvious he's into you. I've seen him with some of the other women he dates. Trust me, I've never seen him look at anyone the way he looks at you."

"That's just lust," I said with a shrug, fighting against the bitter feeling the thought elicited inside.

Zoe shook her head firmly. "It's not just lust. That's obviously there, but it's more. Maybe you should try to talk to him."

As appeared to be the case with all things Tristan, my mouth was ahead of my brain. "Oh, we talked. We made a deal. One month and that's it."

Zoe's eyes widened. "One month of what?"

"Sex."

"You're serious? This was an actual conversation?"

I wasn't up to chatting about the fact I'd pretty much dared him when I announced I'd never had an orgasm with a guy. I wasn't a prude, but I didn't enjoy how insecure that made me feel, so I wasn't going there.

"Uh huh. One month and then..."

I ran out of words because I didn't know what was supposed to happen after that. Hope kept kicking at the doors of my heart.

"And then what?" Zoe asked the obvious question.

I shrugged. "I don't know."

Zoe took a sip of coffee and eyed me thoughtfully. "You like him, he likes you. Why have this silly one month deal?"

"Because," was the best I could offer in explanation. I didn't voice all the doubts crowding my mind. Already, it felt as if the end of that timeline was racing at me.

"I'm going to tell Ethan to pry for me. I'll report back. Give me a few days."

My heart jumped, but I talked it down fast.

"There's no need to do that. That sounds a little too high school for me. Plus, if you talk to Ethan, he might mention it to someone else and then everyone will know."

Zoe rolled her eyes. "Romance at the beginning always has a little high school in it. I don't think we ever get past that silly part. It's more high school to try to hide something from all of your friends. I'm not trying to give you a hard time, just pointing it out."

I put my face in my hands and sighed. "I know," I mumbled. I forced myself to look up because I wasn't going to be that much of a chicken. "Right. It makes it seem all cloak and dagger, which is ridiculous. We're friends and we have all the same friends. I don't know why I'm so weird about it."

"No need to be embarrassed. Hell, I was running around in secret with Ethan, trying to make sure it didn't get out we were together. So I know where you're coming from."

"Yeah, but you kind of had a reason. I don't."

Zoe rolled her eyes. "Yeah, I was screwing my client. That doesn't exactly make it better," she said with a wry laugh. Her laugh faded. "I think maybe you should either put a stop to this or face why you're tiptoeing around."

The idea of no more nights like last night with Tristan made my heart ache and my body feel bereft. Whatever Zoe saw in my face, her gaze softened.

"So you definitely don't want to do that. Well, I say go at it full bore. No hiding, just let it be what it is. Oh, and let me pry. Ethan can get Tristan to talk, and if I ask him to keep his mouth shut, he will. I know he likes to tease, but he's a total softie and he would never do that if he knew it might make you uncomfortable."

I stared at her. Crazy as it was, she had a point. Half the reason this whole thing made me feel squirrely was I didn't do things in half-measures like this. Screw it. There was no need to hide what was happening. I might as well treat Tristan the way I'd treat any guy I was seeing.

"You're right," I said firmly. "I'm being ridiculous. I'll be loud and proud about it. Meanwhile, pry away. Let me know what you find out."

"On it," Zoe replied with a wink.

Chapter Seventeen

TRISTAN

I sat on the bench in the locker room and drained a bottle of water. We'd had a long practice today, made longer with our new player getting into it with Liam during practice. Roddy Shaw was struggling so far to mesh with the team, solely due to his cocky attitude. Confidence in your skills was a must for any of us who played pro sports. I mean, hell, you weren't much use to your team if you didn't have faith in your own ability. Yet, to be part of a team required mutual respect. I was also a firm believer that you never stopped learning when it came to play. I was a much better player than I'd been even a few years ago, in large part due to honing my skills. When you're young, it's easy to falsely believe you're at your peak. At thirty-two, most people would still consider me young. For pro sports, I was about middle age, so to speak.

Roddy was young, yet he swaggered about like he owned the fucking team. The fact Roddy would dare to challenge Liam's calls on plays was mind-boggling. The kid had yet to play an actual game professionally yet, and he thought he was all that. Whatever. Anyway, I was waiting around, figuring Liam might want to grab a beer and blow off his frustration with today's practice.

I heard footsteps and glanced up to find Ethan rounding the row of lockers. He sat down on the bench across from me, sliding down until he was directly in front of me.

"Waiting for Liam?" he asked.

I nodded.

He ran a hand through his damp hair and rolled his eyes. "That Roddy's a cocky bloke, eh?"

I rolled my eyes and tossed my now empty water bottle into the recycling bin in the corner. "That's a nice way to put it. Liam was hot about it, and I don't blame 'im."

"Nah. Me neither. Think Roddy'll last?"

"With Coach?" I asked in return.

Coach Hoffman was an old lion when it

came to pro football. He was one of the best offensive players of his generation. His time had passed, but he was young for a coach, perhaps in his late forties. He'd retired from playing after a car accident that killed his wife and daughter and left him hobbled with injuries. I had total respect for him. Aside from his prowess as a player, he was a no non-sense coach. He had little to no tolerance for any player who didn't ascribe to a team frame of mind. Roddy most certainly did not.

At Ethan's nod, I shrugged. "Dunno. If he keeps up like this, I doubt it. It won't work with this kind of tension on the team. He wants to be captain yesterday, and he's barely out of university. Even if he had more experi-ence, no team would support him as captain. He's a little shit."

Ethan whistled low. "Bloody hell. If you're pissed, that tells me how the rest of the team feels. You and Alex are the two most laidback guys we've got. I heard from him out on the pitch. He's got no time for this bullshit."

"None of us do."

The distinct sound of sneakers on the concrete headed in our direction. We both looked to see Liam coming around the row of lockers. He slid onto the bench near me with a sigh.

"What's up boys?" he asked.

"Figured you might want to grab a beer," I replied.

"I'd bloody love one," he said emphatically.

"Alex around?" Ethan asked.

"Nah, something about Harper's car being in the shop, so he had to go pick her up from work. He took off already," Liam explained.

The three of us stood in unison and walked out. We didn't even need to discuss where we were going. We had a few favorite nearby pubs, or as they were called in the States, bars. We headed for a local brewery nearby and snagged a booth in the corner.

Over burgers and beers, we commiserated with Liam who had the misfortune of clashing most frequently with Roddy by virtue of his position as playmaker.

"Bloody fool thinks he should have input into calling plays because he played my position back up in university," Liam said, his tone incredulous.

Ethan chuckled and snagged a French fry. "We should bet on how long he lasts."

We managed to move on from that with Ethan regaling us with a few amusing stories about Zoe trying to boss around the carpenter handling some renovations on their home. Next thing I knew, he set me back on my heels.

"Oh right, I'm supposed to ask you about Daisy," Ethan said, turning my way. "We saw you two out to dinner the other night. Zoe says it's all hush hush, but she wants me to talk to you."

My mouth actually fell open. I snapped it shut the moment Liam burst out laughing, while I mentally went on lock down, trying not to show he'd rattled me.

Once Liam caught his breath, he shook his head. "Mate, if she told you it was supposed to be hush hush, you've already screwed up."

Ethan looked flummoxed. "How so? I'm just asking."

"Well, I'm here, so now I know too," Liam clarified. He turned his teasing gaze to me. "Having dinner with Daisy, are you now?"

I eyed them both and shrugged, striving for casual in my tone. "Is there a problem with that?"

"Zoe thinks you like her, and she wanted me to find out. In fact, she said she needed me to do some reconnaissance," Ethan explained.

"It's bloody dinner. When did you see us anyway?" I asked, knowing full well if they happened to have seen Daisy and I out, it might have been noticeable that I couldn't keep my eyes off of her. I didn't know what the hell to do about her. Nothing about Daisy and the way she affected me made sense. Instead of getting her out of my system, the more time I spent with her, the more I obsessed about her. The whole thing was morphing into the epic disaster I'd worried about. I couldn't reason my way out of my feelings.

Liam drained his beer and threw a cheeky grin my way. "Sounding a tad cranky, Tristan."

I wasn't going to let him bait me, so I merely rolled my eyes and looked back to Ethan.

"At that new fusion place last week, whatever the hell it's called. Zoe thinks, well, she thinks all kinds of things. I think she might be a feeling a tad protective of Daisy."

"What do you mean?" I asked. Like a bloody idiot. I didn't need to further this line of conversation, but I couldn't seem to stop myself.

Ethan eyed me for a beat. "Well, she thinks it won't be cool if you do your usual thing with Daisy. She said Daisy's not like that, and she's our friend."

Bloody hell. Just what I needed. Our mutual friends nosing into this.

"What the hell do you mean, my usual thing?"

Liam, never one to hold back, piped up. "Mate, you've said for as long as I've known you that you don't do relationships. You treat sex like a doctor's appointment, except maybe more fun. I think you think you've got it all worked out, but if you ask me half the women you have your arrangements with probably want more, but they go along with it because of who you are. Daisy's been on the hunt for something serious for as long as I've known her. Olivia's actually said she's been a little worried because Daisy hasn't even been dating anymore recently. She thinks Daisy's depressed about the whole thing."

I looked from Liam and Ethan only to find Ethan nodding along. Oh fuck. This was not what I needed. I also took offense at the implication about me.

"I'm not some fucking arse who takes advantage of women. I go out of my way to make sure things are clear right up front. That's a hell of a lot more respectful than some bullshit guys pull," I said, trying to keep the annoyance and defensiveness out of my tone.

"Oh, it's not like that. You know me, I understand. Hell, I used to be a bit like you, although I think I had more fun," Liam said with a chuckle.

Ethan rolled his eyes. "I don't think you've done anything wrong. I just think you might want to be careful. Daisy might have expectations, and well, she's our friend."

I glanced between them again and bit back a sigh. I couldn't fucking believe two of my best mates were having a little chat with me about making sure I took care of Daisy. I'd cut off my arm before I'd hurt her. The very idea of it made me sick. This train of thought sent a thread of unease through me. I hadn't made her any promises. In fact, I'd even put a time limit on us. One month, which was now down to twenty days since I'd tossed out that salvo. Thinking about how much time we had left made me irritable. I was already mentally bargaining with myself, contemplating adding another month. Maybe that's what we needed to snuff out the need nearly burning me alive.

Twenty days felt like nothing. I knew without pondering, it wouldn't be enough time with her. Yet, trying to think past what that meant made my brain fill with static.

I gave myself a mental shake and endeavored to gloss this over with Liam and Ethan, all the while wondering what the hell I was doing. I left the pub stirred up and restless after promising them I'd never hurt Daisy.

A promise I wasn't so sure I could keep and one that made me wonder if my own heart was at as much risk as hers.

Chapter Eighteen

DAISY

"Excuse me?" I asked, caught flat-footed by the doctor's question.

"I asked if you'd like to have dinner with me," Jeff Miller explained.

I was at a meeting at the hospital, reviewing the data on a different research study than the one Tristan was temporarily covering. Dr. Jeff Miller was rather handsome with his dark blonde hair, brown eyes and chiseled features. I'd bet he spent plenty of time at the gym too. I stared over at him, thinking that a few weeks ago, I'd have been flattered. Not that I felt a spark with him. I didn't. Not even a little, but he was bright and handsome. Before Tristan, I'd have thought he was worth getting to know and would have wondered if things could develop into something real with him.

Instead, all I could think about was Tristan. We'd had another night together last night. Right here, right now, right after a decent man asked me out to dinner, I got hot inside at the mere thought of Tristan. He was proving his point again and again and again. Last night, he'd left me boneless with his mouth and fingers. Then he'd driven me right to the edge and over again with a long, slow bout of him buried inside of me.

I couldn't even contemplate trying to see someone else. Yet, I was starting to get more than a little worried about my heart. With a mental shove, I nudged my thoughts off that track and managed a polite smile in Jeff's direction.

"Thank you, but no."

Jeff didn't miss a beat and nodded. "Understood. I suppose you have some kind of rule about not mixing research and pleasure."

I shrugged and smiled ruefully. "Something like that."

It wasn't a blatant lie. I had always tried to walk that line carefully, but it wasn't a hard and fast rule. It's just that I couldn't exactly say, "Actually, I'm fucking Dr. Wells and he's ruined me for every other man. Permanently probably."

Did I mention I was in over my head? Falling so far, so deep, I feared I might drown.

Jeff was gracious enough not to make it awkward, and we carried on with our conversation. I was showing him something in the data system when there was a sharp knock on the door.

"Come in," Jeff called.

The door opened and Dr. Horton stood there with Tristan.

Dr. Horton was my primary contact here at the hospital, yet he'd been on leave for an extended period of time. I hadn't quite expected him back yet.

He glanced from Jeff to me with a beaming smile. With his round glasses, his warm blue eyes and his generally jolly manner, it was impossible not to return his smile.

"Daisy, I thought we'd find you here. I was just telling Tristan it would be helpful for him to join your meeting with Jeff. As I'm sure you've noticed, the study he's managing has been running like a dream," Dr. Horton said as he stepped to me.

I stood from my chair and reached to shake his hand, but he clapped me on the shoulder instead. I felt Tristan's eyes on me and looked up with a carefully polite smile. I only hoped my calm, professional façade belied the wild beat of my heart and the flutters spinning in my belly.

"Hello Daisy," Tristan said with a nod, staying right where he'd stepped beside the round table.

"I didn't expect to see you back so soon," I said to Dr. Horton. "Of course, I'm thrilled, but I hope you didn't cut your time off short because you missed work so much."

Dr. Horton stepped back and flashed me a wry smile. "Ah, you do know I like my work. Actually, my wife got laid low with one of those horrible intestinal viruses on our cruise, and all she wanted to do was come home. We decided to try a different trip next year, so I'm back to work early. Not to worry though. I did have a full three months off. I've only returned a month early." He paused and glanced among us. "So how are things going with this trial?" he asked, looking to Jeff.

"As you mentioned earlier," Jeff started, obviously in reference to another conversation with Dr. Horton, "...we've had some challenges with the screening tools for this one. My team is also experiencing some frustrations with handling the two different computer systems."

I stayed quiet. My opinion on the matter was Jeff didn't appear to be insisting on the data entry needed for the medication trial. Seeing as he was part of a research project, to say that was missing the point didn't even come close. It was a non-negotiable issue. This hadn't come up with the trial Tristan was managing, but then I could guess Tristan to be a strong leader. Jeff had more of a cajoling manner, which I imagined led staff to think they had wiggle room.

It annoyed me to no end that I respected Tristan so much. Aside from the fact he could melt me with a look these days, he was too much of what I wanted. I politely listened as Dr. Horton, Jeff and Tristan chatted about a few issues. My presence wasn't really necessary, but I didn't feel like I could leave. Meanwhile, my mind wandered to Tristan and what it meant to have Dr. Horton back. We only had two weeks left of our agreed upon month, but I'd known I'd be seeing him once a week for the next six weeks. I hated thinking about it, but I'd been foolishly hanging onto those extra weeks, thinking maybe I'd get more than the month with him.

Oh God. This was bad.

"Daisy?"

Dr. Horton's voice broke through my wandering thoughts.

"Yes?"

"I was hoping you didn't mind continuing your weekly meetings with Tristan and Jeff for another few weeks. I've got some other projects to focus on and tons of catch up to do."

My heart did a little dance. I didn't mind meeting with Jeff, but I was downright ec-static to have a few more chances to see Tristan once our allotted month came to an end. That's how bad off I was.

"Of course not," I said, focusing to keep my tone level and my expression nothing but bland and polite.

"Excellent then. You know if you need me, all you have to do is call," Dr. Horton replied with another wide smile.

He said his goodbyes, leaving me alone with Jeff and Tristan. I glanced between them. "Was there anything else we needed to cover?" I asked, glancing toward Jeff.

"I don't think so. I'll follow up with my team on the data issues and make sure they stay on top of it." He paused and looked to Tristan. "In case you didn't know, Dr. Knight is off limits," he said with a wink and a wry smile.

Well, this was a little awkward, along with infuriating. Before I had a chance to open my mouth, Tristan's eyes darkened and he glared at Jeff.

"Apologize," he said sharply.

Jeff who had just shown himself to be one of those 'boys will be boys' assholes looked taken aback. "Dude, I was just joking. It was a compliment, really."

I eyed him. "Sorry, but no. I'm here in a professional capacity. There's no reason for you to assume anything, particularly not that it should be announced I'm off limits. You asked me to dinner. I said no. End of conversation. If you thought it wasn't about you, you can reconsider."

Tristan's eyes flicked from me back to Jeff. "Obviously, Dr. Knight can take care of herself. We treat all professionals professionally here. Keep that in mind in the future," he said curtly.

I sensed he wanted to say more, but he didn't. His jaw was clenched and his shoulders were tense. Jeff held his gaze and then looked to me. "My apologies."

I nodded and turned away. Tristan was right behind me, opening the door and gesturing me through. We didn't speak and started walking in the direction of his office, which was two floors up and on the opposite side of the hospital. I could feel the tension emanating from Tristan, but he didn't say a word. We waited in silence for the elevator and then stepped in. When he hit the button for a different floor, I glanced his way.

"Your office is on floor three."

He finally looked at me, and my heart gave a hard thump. His eyes were dark, and I could see a muscle ticking in his jaw. He glanced up to the screen above the elevator door, indicating what floor we were passing. Abruptly he hit the stop button, and the elevator whispered to a stop. Before I could ask him what he was doing, he spun to me. My back bumped against the wall as he crowded against me. The air around us instantly felt alive with a pounding, intense need. His eyes collided with mine, his gaze searching.

"Tristan, what are you..."

My words were lost in his kiss. He fit his mouth over mine, sweeping his tongue deeply inside. There was no slow build up to this kiss. Inside of mere seconds, I was burning up inside, flexing against him, my hands greedily yanking his shirt out of his slacks, so I could feel him. I groaned into his mouth once my palm slid up over the hard planes of his chest, his skin hot and sleek. He tore his mouth free, and I gulped in air. One of his hands was laced roughly into my hair, the other palm cupping my breast.

Inside the enclosed space of the elevator, it felt as if we were all alone in the world. The sound of our breath heaving filled the space. My heartbeat drummed through my body, each beat feeding the crescendo of need rising inside of me. His forehead fell to mine as he eased his grip on my hair and sifted through it.

"Miller asked you out," he said, a statement rather than a question.

I opened my eyes to find his right there, boring into mine. I nodded, just barely.

"I said no," I whispered.

I have no idea why I felt the need to explain that, but I did. It's not like Tristan and I were serious. He'd made the fact we weren't perfectly clear. Yet, I was the one who'd asked him to stay exclusive if only for this month. I felt he had to know I would honor that.

I could hardly bear to tell him the truth—there was no way I could even imagine being with anyone other than him even beyond the end of this month. I wanted more, so much more, but it didn't matter. I'd walked into this with my eyes wide open. We had a month for me to have as many orgasms as I could manage. Though my body was thrumming with need, I wasn't lost in it yet. This moment felt intense, raw and intimate in a different way.

His eyes searched mine. I could feel the steady beat of his heart against my palm. Meanwhile, mine pounded so hard, I was quite certain he could hear it.

"I don't have any say, but I'm glad you said no," he murmured.

"Why?"

That one word literally jumped out of my mouth, so rushed was it to be heard. He was silent for a moment that stretched so long, I ached inside and out. I wanted him. So desperately and in so many ways I wasn't supposed to want him. If only it were purely physical, it would all be so much simpler.

"Because I don't like thinking about you with anyone else," he finally said.

His voice was low and gruff and sent a curl of warmth around my heart. I shouldn't have savored it, but I liked knowing he was jealous.

"You said one month."

Again, my mouth was about ten steps ahead of my brain. I didn't really want to debate this right now.

"I said we'd reassess in a month," he replied, his eyes never breaking from mine.

I swallowed, trying to control the wild beat of my heart and the hope clamoring to be heard inside. There were so many things I wanted to say, but none of them made sense. Not right now. For once, my brain caught up and managed to shush me.

"Oh," was all I could manage.

With the air heavy with need, the intimacy shimmering around us made me feel exposed. I started to get anxious. As if he could sense the shift, he dipped his head and started dropping kisses along my neck. Hot shivers raced through me, and I immediately forgot everything but this moment—his hard body pressed to mine, his cock nestled against my core, and his lips blazing fire along my skin.

The elevator suddenly started moving again. At the subtle jolt of motion, he lifted his head.

"Bloody hell," he muttered.

He stepped back, and I quickly stepped away from where I'd been leaning against the wall. We both quickly adjusted our clothing. I thought I had everything in place until he reached over and pulled the edge of my collar over. I flushed at the brush of his fingers on my skin.

I looked up quickly, colliding with his gaze—hot, dark and locked to me. He didn't say a word, but something flashed in the depths of his eyes. The elevator came to a stop, and he quickly stepped back, dropping his hand. The doors whisked open, and a cheerful nurse stood there with an elderly woman in a wheelchair.

"Well, hello there Dr. Wells," the nurse said as she wheeled her patient into the elevator. Once they were inside, the nurse turned around, so the woman in the wheelchair was situated between Tristan and I. Without being asked, he leaned over and adjusted the footrests on the chair.

The woman glanced up and bestowed a smile on him. "Aren't you a polite boy?"

I bit my lip to keep from laughing. She swung to me. She had curly gray hair, sparkling blue eyes and an impish smile.

"Well, wouldn't you agree?" she asked me.

"Of course. Dr. Wells is definitely a polite boy."

Her gaze bounced between us before her impish grin widened. "He's no Dr. Wells to you, dear."

My cheeks got hot, and I couldn't keep my eyes from flicking to Tristan who was actually biting the inside of his cheek to keep from laughing. When I didn't say anything, she shrugged.

"I'm old and that counts for a lot of experience. I know when I sense something. Plus, your lips are puffy. I'd bet polite Dr. Wells was kissing you, or perhaps you started it. You do look a bit bossy."

The whole thing was so ridiculous, I started laughing. She laughed right along with me. When I caught my breath, I looked down at her. "Anything else you'd like to tell me about myself?"

She cocked her head to the side. "No dear. He's yummy, and he likes you."

At that, the elevator came to a whispering stop. The nurse was laughing softly as she rolled past us. Tristan caught my eyes, barely holding back his grin.

"This is my floor too. With Dr. Horton back, they put me here for the last month I'll be here."

I simply nodded. When I didn't move, he arched a brow. "Aren't we meeting?"

Sweet hell. I'd completely forgotten we actually had work to do. I gathered my dignity and followed him down the hall, wondering if perhaps we could lock the door and forget the rest of the world for a bit.

Chapter Nineteen

TRISTAN

I was wound tight inside. I had perfectly respectable, professional reasons to remind Daisy we were supposed to have our weekly meeting. Our meeting was entirely unnecessary, and I damn well knew it. The data she liked to review weekly was all up to date. There wasn't much to discuss. I'd come to learn she was on the bossy side when it came to the medication trials she managed. I actually loved that about her. If only because it turned me on.

I could've just let her carry on with her day. But I needed her. *Now.*

My cock had been rock hard since we'd entered the elevator. I was quite grateful everyone who passed by us in this wing of the hospital was either looking at their phone, or barely acknowledging us. Daisy walked beside me, her low heels clicking rhythmically on the floor. Once again, she was dressed quite appropriately. She wore a fitted black skirt that flared just above her knees, paired with a fitted cream blouse and kitten heels, which she seemed to favor. Of course, more than a cursory glance and it was impossible not to notice how the blouse strained slightly at the buttons between her breasts.

I'd bet money she was wearing a sheer silk bra with a thong to match. I'd come to learn she tended to match her lingerie with whatever she was wearing. That would mean cream silk today. Just thinking about it sent blood straight to my already hard cock and made my mouth water.

It felt like we walked forever to reach my office. I tried, oh I bloody tried, to stay in control. I closed the door behind her and locked it. I turned to see her setting her purse down on the table. She leaned over to brush something off the chair closest to her, giving me a glimpse of the valley between her breasts. The reins slipped through my fingers. I was standing right in front of her when she straightened.

Her eyes widened, and her breath drew in

sharply. I managed to gather some control and held still. A fucking miracle with her this close. On the heels of a breath, I stepped to her and cupped her bottom, bringing her flush to me. Her cheeks pinkened, and her breath came in short pants.

"I want you," I nearly growled.

Her eyes flicked up to mine. "What are you waiting for?"

At the sound of her voice, raspy with passion and tinged with her bossiness, I dipped my head and picked up right where I'd left off in the elevator. Only now I was near out of my mind with need mingling with emotion swirling inside of me. I yanked at her blouse as my lips, teeth and tongue made their way down into the valley between her breasts. The buttons gave way easily, and as expected, her bra was sheer cream silk. Her nipples were taut and pink through the silk. I laved my tongue over one and then the other, savoring her moans and the roll of her hips against me.

Fuck. I needed her, and I needed her now. I spun her around, shoving her skirt up as I did. Her foot caught on the chair leg, and I couldn't have planned it better. She caught her balance on the table as I reflexively steadied her hips. As it was, her gorgeous bottom was exposed with her skirt flipped up over it. When I trailed my fingertip along the strip of silk that rested between her cheeks, she placed her other palm on the table and arched into my touch. The silk between her thighs was soaked.

I was usually a man who took my time. I could only manage that sometimes with Daisy. She was too tempting, too delicious, too much of everything I wanted. I hooked a finger over the edge of her panties, yanking them down swiftly where they pooled around her ankles. With the kick of a foot, she knocked them out of the way. I knelt down and stroked up her thighs with my palms, widening them slightly as I did.

Her pussy, pink and glistening from her juices was too much for me to resist. I dragged my tongue along its cleft, my fingers digging into her hips as I held her still. I meant to make her come so hard she saw stars, but she was bossy and impatient. She wiggled her hips amidst a few groans.

"Tristan, no... Oh God."

I drew back. "No?" I asked as I sank a finger into her channel. It clenched around me.

"I want you inside," she murmured on the heels of another moan.

"But I am," I countered as I stretched her with another finger and stroked into her.

"It's not enough," she said, more strongly this time.

"You're sure about that?" I teased with a swirl of my thumb over her clit.

"Just...fuck...me," she murmured between gasps as her hips rolled back into my touch.

I found I didn't mind being ordered around by Daisy at all. In a flash, I straightened and freed my cock, not even bothering to shove my slacks down. I gripped it in my fist and dragged the head back and forth in her drenched folds.

She glanced over her shoulder, her wide brown eyes dark and her lips pink and plump. Damn me straight to hell, but with her hair in a tidy twist and her professional skirt shoved up over her ass, I wanted to fuck her a thousand times over anywhere we shouldn't be. For example, here in my borrowed office at the hospital when I was supposed to be discussing research data with her.

I held her gaze and sank inside of her in a slow surge, burying myself to the hilt. I couldn't say I was thinking—at all—but if I'd meant to drag this out in any way, that became impossible with the little moan she let out. Her bottom arched up, almost begging me. I started to move and inside of seconds, I was drumming into her, pressure bundling inside as she rolled her hips back into every stroke, riding my cock as if she'd been made for it. I reached in front and dragged my finger in a swirl over her swollen clit. She cried out, my name coming in between gasps and moans. I barely heard with my own release thundering through me so hard, I was weak at the end of it.

I had to catch my balance with my hand curled over the edge of the table and the other gripping her hip. Her head fell forward, and our breath heaved in unison. When the haze in my brain cleared, I dropped a few kisses in the dip of her spine before straightening and reluctantly drawing out of her. It was the craziest thing, but it didn't matter I'd just spent myself inside of her—all I wanted was to stay with her like that, buried deep inside and connected. It transcended pure physical pleasure, and I didn't even know how to face it.

I grabbed a handful of tissues out of the box on the table and wiped between her thighs. She was so wet, the entire insides of her thighs were damp with her fluids and now mingling with mine. The only relief it offered was the knowledge she was as far gone as I was when it came to the need between us. It was a living, breathing force of its own. I wiped myself off and buttoned my slacks with one hand while I retrieved her discarded underwear. She glanced down with a puzzled look when I leaned over and nudged her ankle.

"I'm assuming you'd like to put these back on," I explained.

"Well, yeah, but what are you doing?"

"Helping."

With a low laugh, she lifted one ankle and then the other. I slid her silk panties up over her hips and smoothed her skirt in place. When I straightened and met her eyes, my heart started to thud—hard and fast—against my ribs.

Chapter Twenty

DAISY

"Geez Daisy, what's up with you?" Olivia asked, her way too perceptive gaze swinging to me.

We were at Desert Isle Coffee waiting for Harper to arrive. It was a rainy evening in Seattle, and a guy I'd been interested in a few months ago had stopped by our table to chat. Apparently, I wasn't friendly enough.

"What do you mean?" I countered.

Olivia took a sip of her coffee and brushed a loose curl out of her eyes. With her dark curly hair, porcelain skin and green eyes, Olivia was lovely. She had that whole sexy librarian vibe going too with her glasses and prim attitude. She was actually pretty laid back, but so serious about her work it was easy to miss that about her if you didn't know her well. We'd grown up together in a small town outside of Seattle, so she'd been my bestie forever. I was hoping she wouldn't notice anything, but then that wouldn't make sense because she and Harper knew me better than anyone did.

"Well, you thought he was totally hot a few months ago. He's being all nice and asks you to dinner, and you turn him down? That's not like you. Come to think of it, you haven't dated anyone in months. What happened to your plan to find the right guy?"

I bought myself a minute or two by adding a dash of creamer to my coffee. I considered Zoe's point that hiding what was happening with Tristan wasn't doing myself any favors. I was usually the pushy one with my friends—wanting everyone to find the love of their lives. I'd come to doubt the possibility so much so for myself, I was frustrated and feeling defensive.

I finally looked back over at her and steeled myself. "Well, you've been saying forever maybe I should stop looking so hard," I hedged.

I was instantly annoyed with myself. I wasn't a chicken and wasn't going to keep slinking about. Another gulp of coffee and then I eyed her again. Unlike me, Olivia didn't tend to jump right in with her opinion, so she was still waiting patiently.

"I'm, uh..."

What the hell are you and Tristan doing? Screwing? Dating?

Gah! I don't know.

I had to explain somehow.

"Tristan and I are sort of seeing each other," I blurted out.

Olivia's eyes widened and then narrowed. "So that's what Liam meant."

"What are you talking about?"

"Oh, the other night he asked me if I knew about you and Tristan. Because I had no idea..." She paused and pinned me with an accusing glare. "...I told him he was crazy. Then his mom called and I forgot all about asking him what he meant."

"Oh great. That means Tristan's talking about it."

Anxiety tightened in my chest. I didn't like worrying about what might've been said. I had nothing to hide, so I reasoned it didn't matter if Tristan had said anything about us.

"Why would it matter if he was?" Olivia asked.

I idly twirled the end of a damp lock of hair around my finger. I'd forgotten my rain jacket today and had gotten wet walking from my office to here.

"I don't know. It just seemed better if we kept it quiet. But then that makes it seem even weirder."

"Okay," Olivia said slowly. "How about you fill me in here? Are you guys *dating-dating* or something else?"

"Um, I think something else."

Something else is one way to put it. You've agreed to a month of orgasms. Nothing more.

Olivia was quiet. The bell above the door jingled, and I glanced over to see Harper entering. She gave us a wave and headed to the counter.

After another quiet moment, Olivia's eyes narrowed. "Is it weird because you and Tristan want different things?"

"What do you mean?" I asked, knowing perfectly well what she meant.

"Oh you know, maybe the fact you've been on a public mission to find the right guy, while Tristan has always been totally clear he's not interested in a relationship."

My stomach churned and my heart hurt a little. This was the thing I didn't want to think about, much less talk about. I started to get that squirrelly feeling inside, but I pushed back against it. Fuck that. I wasn't going to be all wimpy about this. No matter what happened in the end, this was a good thing. I didn't have to wonder if I had the capacity to have an orgasm with a man. I knew enough about relationships to know I could find someone else. I might have to take some radical steps to make sure my heart didn't break after Tristan and I ended our little arrangement, but even that was worth it.

I took a fortifying gulp of coffee and eyed Olivia. "Maybe so, but I decided to go for it anyway. I guess I figured it'll be all for the best if we burn out this crazy chemistry between us and move on as friends."

Harper arrived at the tail end of my sentence, her questioning blue gaze bouncing between us. "Crazy chemistry?"

Now that I'd let the cat out of the bag so to speak, I was so relieved I was embracing it. "Too long/didn't read version: Tristan and I are getting it on. No, we're not serious. I know what I want and he wants are different, but... crazy chemistry," I offered with a shrug.

Harper slipped into the chair at an angle from me and nodded slowly. "Okay then. Did I miss anything else?"

Olivia eyed me and then looked to Harper. "I don't think this is a good idea. It's got disaster written all over it," she said firmly.

"Oh my God, don't be ridiculous," I protested.

"I'm not being ridiculous. You're my friend, and I don't want to see you get hurt. I think Tristan's great and if you ask me..."

Harper shook her head at Olivia, her pointed gaze silencing Olivia with a glance. Harper with her warm blue eyes, glossy brown hair and usually quiet manner hid her steely strength. She'd had her own tragedy over five years ago when she was raped, but she was so far past that, I sometimes found it hard to believe it had ever happened. She was happily married to Alex Gordon, yet another player for the Seattle Stars. He loved Harper so much, I tended to feel as if I was constantly interrupting an intimate moment with them. Anyway, back to my point. Harper was the center of reason for all of us in our circle. She had little tolerance for overblown responses to anything. I was usually the brunt of her firm redirection, so for the moment, I enjoyed Olivia occupying that position.

"Daisy can do what she wants to do. If it means she gets hurt, that's what it means," Harper said firmly.

"Yeah, but I want her to find what she wants. I mean, I'm sure Tristan is amazing in bed, if the rumors are anything to go on, but come on Harper. You know this won't end well. It wouldn't be so bad if we weren't all friends," Olivia said with a sigh.

After a sip of coffee, Harper glanced to me. "How do you think that will go??

"What?"

"The awkward-try-to-be-friends thing," Harper clarified.

I shrugged. "Truth is we've been dealing with that all year. Things got a little hot and heavy when I went to that away game with you last year," I said, glancing to Olivia. "Since then, I've been avoiding him. I finally decided it wasn't worth it anymore."

Olivia huffed and glared at me. "Wow, you've been hiding this for a year?"

"It was one kiss, okay? The way you're responding is only reinforcing why I didn't say anything. Look, maybe it's stupid, but I figured I'd rather get him out of my system than keep trying to avoid him."

"I also think Tristan likes you," Harper added.

That stupid little sprout of hope in my heart just wouldn't die. Comments like this from Harper only made it wave around a little more. While I was trying to beat back the feeling, Olivia did me a favor.

"What do you mean?" she asked.

"Just that. I mean, whenever we're somewhere with both of you, he can hardly keep his eyes off of you. He reminds me a little bit of Alex and the way he used to approach relationships," Harper explained.

"What do you mean?" I asked, parroting Olivia.

"He's got this idea he can compartmentalize everything like that. I think it only works if you don't really care about someone. The way he looks at you is about more than sex and has been for years. I totally get why Olivia might be worried, but I won't be surprised if things turn out differently."

I wanted to jump up and down in my chair and hug Harper. I held myself back because I wasn't quite ready to make a fool of myself. Olivia seemed to be stunned into silence. I took a sip of coffee and glanced between them.

"It would be great if you could just be there for me if I do get hurt and trust I walked into this with my eyes wide open," I said.

Olivia smiled ruefully and leaned over to squeeze my shoulders in a half hug. "Of course. You know I'm the worrier, but you're a big girl and I know you'll come out fine no matter what."

Conversation moved on and later that evening I wrapped myself in a fluffy robe, planning to settle in for a night of hot chocolate and television. It was still raining outside. I was walking from the kitchen into the living room when the doorbell rang. I hadn't been expecting anyone, so I was curious. When I opened the door, Tristan stood there, his dark hair damp from the rain.

Chapter Twenty-One

TRISTAN

I strode down the hallway after finishing up a meeting with Dr. Horton. With me back to practice and our season starting soon, this interim situation since my knee injury last year was winding to a close, so we had plenty to cover before I finished up here entirely. My mind spun to last night. I hadn't had plans to see Daisy. Hell, I'd told her I was busy with work, which had been the truth. I was busy tying up loose ends, so I could hand the reins back to Dr. Horton. But as appeared to be the case nightly now, I found myself heading over to her place once I was done. I hadn't wanted to go home to my flat. The idea of not being with her elicited a restless feeling I didn't like.

Even though I was uncomfortable with how I felt about Daisy, Daisy herself was the only relief from my discomfort. Beyond the fact we all but went up in flames whenever we were together, I enjoyed her company. Last night, I hadn't been able to resist untying her robe and lifting her onto the kitchen counter before burying myself inside of her. It was that bad. Hell, she'd opened the door in a robe and elephant slippers of all things. Her hair had been pulled back in a messy ponytail. It was fair to say she wasn't trying to be sexy. I'd taken one look and wanted her so fiercely I'd barely gotten past saying hello.

After that, she'd fallen asleep half on my lap while we were watching some sci-fi show. That was another thing that made me half crazy. I'd never have guessed she'd enjoy the same shows I did. I didn't watch a ton of television. I didn't have time for the most part, but when I did I wanted pure entertainment and loved sci-fi movies and the like. Who'd have guessed Daisy was a fan too? With her predilection for romance and her cheery disposition, I'd have pegged her as preferring romantic comedies or dramas. She'd wrinkled her nose when I pointed that out and informed me I was stereotyping her. She continued to surprise me in little and big ways.

I'd carried her to bed after she dozed off. I was becoming altogether too comfortable falling asleep and waking up beside her. I was also hyper-aware of the end of the month I'd allotted for us. I recalled that I'd told her we'd reassess. Just thinking about it made me shy away inside.

I rounded the corner in the hallway and glanced up to see Jeff Miller heading my way. I was instantly annoyed. He'd pissed me off the other day. If I'd been thinking clearly about anything to do with Daisy, I might've recognized much of my anger stemmed from purely irrational jealousy.

Oh, he'd been a typical sexist prick with his joke about Daisy being off limits. That kind of comment just wouldn't be made about a man in her role. Even if I weren't tangled up skin to skin with her almost nightly now, I'd have considered it disrespectful and unprofessional. Yet, I'd practically seen red to hear he'd even asked her out. He glanced up and caught my eyes.

"Hey there, Tristan," he said casually as he reached me and came to a stop.

Unless I wanted to be blatantly rude, I

couldn't just walk on by him as I wanted. I forced my legs to a stop and nodded tightly.

"Meeting with Dr. Horton?" I asked.

"Of course. So with him back, you'll be finishing up here soon, right?"

I nodded, grateful I wasn't a typically chatty guy.

Jeff eyed me for a minute. "So, no offense meant the other day about Daisy. I didn't see the harm in asking her out to dinner. Hell, she's flat gorgeous. I mean, I'm betting you'd like to see her naked too," he said with a low chuckle.

Okay, I was usually a calm guy. I usually wouldn't care in the least if another guy noticed a woman I was seeing. Hell, I was so *not* territorial about women, most I'd had arrangements with saw other people. My only boundaries were no expectations for something serious and no public announcements about our status. Being a pro sports player, I bloody hated the media attention to every breath we took. I sure as hell wasn't interested in women who were looking to get laid only so they could trot it out in the media.

In short, I didn't get jealous and I didn't care when I parted on friendly terms with anyone I'd been seeing. Even when Renee got a little weird about things at the end there, I chalked it up to nothing more than that and moved on.

Daisy was another matter. To hear Jeff make a casual joke about any man wanting to see her naked nearly led me to clock him. I was so fucking angry, my saving grace was the years of discipline honed in me from playing pro. Once the fury dissipated slightly—just barely, really—I actually glanced up and down the hallway and contemplated if I could get away with roughing him up.

I have fucking lost my mind. I'm actually debating whether it's worth starting a fight—a bloody fight—over Daisy.

I gave myself a mental shake. I wasn't that kind of bloke—a foolish, hotheaded idiot who lost it over a girl. But I couldn't let this slide.

Though I hadn't said a word, Jeff's gaze went from an obnoxious, knowing look to one of trepidation. I eyed him for a long moment.

"I already asked you to apologize once," I said in a low voice.

He looked at me uneasily. "Look, man. Just a joke. She's not here to hear it, so no harm done. She's beautiful, and I didn't see any problem with noticing that," he finally said with a slight shrug.

Fucking asshole.

I was still so angry, it took most of my discipline not to punch him. I clenched my fists and tucked them in my pockets. "She deserves to be treated with respect. Obviously you don't understand that concept. Dr. Knight is the lead researcher on multiple studies we handle here. Aside from the fact all women should be treated with respect and not debased with bullshit like what you just spewed, she's about ten times smarter than you as far as I can tell. Back the fuck off and know that I'll be letting Horton know about this."

I didn't wait for his reply and spun away, walking swiftly down the hallway to the elevators.

———

Later that afternoon, I leaned against the goal post and guzzled a bottle of water. We were just finishing up practice, and I was close to exhaustion. I'd thrown myself into practice, needing the physical activity to nudge my thoughts off of Daisy and how unsettled I was over her. I was still irritable about Jeff's comments, mostly because of my own reaction to them. It sucked, but being a man meant you learned many, many, many men were sexist jerks. As it was, I shouldn't be so bloody mad about Jeff's comments about Daisy. Yet, I was.

I was acutely aware of why. The reality that Jeff noticed her and found her attractive shouldn't have been the least bit surprising to me. Daisy was beautiful. With her bright honey gold hair, her wide brown eyes, her endearing lopsided smile, and her curves that went on forever, I was confident plenty of men noticed her. Hell, I'd noticed her the first time I met her. The more time I spent with her, the more that attention had grown into a fierce desire for her. I'd only barely tamped it down due to our friendship and the awareness she'd wanted more than what I wanted.

Then, I'd gone and given in to the urge to kiss her. If she hadn't spent the subsequent year avoiding me, I was fairly certain we'd have arrived in this very place much sooner. The desire between us burned so hot and fast, it was a replicating force. Nothing seemed to take the edge off my need for her. Even when I'd just spent myself and was still buried inside of her, all I could think of was how fucking good it felt. How right.

Case in point. Right now, I should be focused on the team. We'd had a grueling practice and most of us were bloody annoyed with Roddy. I figured he was on his last shot before Coach told management to go to hell and trade him. While I was able to focus when I was actually playing, once I wasn't, my mind spun to Daisy.

Fuck me. I pushed off the goal post and glanced to Alex. I'd stopped to chat with him on the way to the locker rooms. While Liam was mostly stuck dealing with Roddy's cocky attitude, the kid had been foolish enough today to offer defensive pointers to Alex.

Alex slung a towel over his shoulder and stepped to my side. "Eh, he's enough of a problem now, Coach shall have to do something. As for me, he can jabber at me all he wants and I'll just keep ignoring him," Alex said with a shrug in response to whatever the hell I'd said a minute ago.

That how pathetic I was. The second I started thinking about Daisy, I lost track of everything else.

Alex, having known me for years and being damn perceptive, eyed me and cocked his head to the side.

"What's up with you? I know your knee's up to speed because I can see it in your play. You're not favoring it at all. If anything, you seem a tad faster than you were before your injury."

We began walking slowly toward the locker room. I twirled the now-empty water bottle in my hand, not replying to Alex because I didn't have a good answer.

Alex let me be for a few seconds and then prodded me. "So?"

I shrugged. "Nothing. Long practice today, and Roddy's annoying as hell."

I glanced to my side to see Alex arch a brow and shrug. He wouldn't push because he wasn't that kind of guy. We headed to the showers. I let the steaming water pound over me longer than usual while I stewed over Daisy. Yet again, we hadn't made plans tonight. I wanted to see her. *Needed* to see her. All the while wishing my need for her wasn't quite so fierce. Trying to shove it away only seemed to heighten it.

Chapter Twenty-Two

DAISY

"You're coming to dinner, right?" Olivia asked the second I answered her call.

I glanced at the clock above my office door and then at the spreadsheet I'd been reviewing. I'd been deep in data all today. It was actually something I loved. The precise nature of it, the answers it could give me, how satisfying it felt when it was organized and told me something good—maybe it was crazy, but it was what I loved. I'd known from the start of medical school that I wanted to do research. Medical research had saved us in so many ways. Most people today didn't even have to think about small pox or polio because those diseases, which had killed swathes of humanity in eras before, were largely eradicated. I was passionate about the fact I felt like medical research had lost its way in the era of profit. The research company I worked for was small, but embodied everything that mattered to me. It was a non-profit, and we focused on preventative medication trials.

As it was, I'd had a great day filled with data, but dinner sounded nice. "I didn't know we were having dinner, but I'm game. When, where and who?" I asked in return.

"Me and Liam, Harper and Alex, Zoe and Ethan." She paused, and I could practically hear her wondering if this was a good idea. "And Tristan. If you come, then you too," she said quickly.

It was like a couples dinner then, and the first dinner with all of my closest friends where the fact Tristan and I were doing whatever the hell it was we were doing was public knowledge amongst our friends. My heart gave a little squeeze. The part that hurt was the knowledge we might be there and we might sort of be together, but not really. Oh God. The end of our month was coming too fast and was also too far away. Trying to gracefully manage the pending end of this would put my heart to the test.

"I'll be there. You forgot the where and when," I said quickly.

I couldn't dwell on what Olivia might be worrying about, and I wasn't going to hide anymore.

"Oh right. Six o'clock at Thai Paradise," she added.

"See you then."

I hung up quickly and spent the next half hour finishing up everything I'd been working on, so I had a good starting point next week. With it being Friday, before this whole thing with Tristan had started, I might've worked over the weekend. I had no intention of doing that this weekend. He'd been spending every night with me lately. We only had this weekend left before we had to 'reassess' as he'd declared we would do at the end of our month together.

Not much later, I pushed through the doorway into Thai Paradise. The restaurant was an old favorite of mine and Olivia's from back when we were in med school together. It was quick and delicious and perfect for late night of studying. I pushed the hood back from my rain jacket and took it off before shaking it. The drizzle earlier today had turned into true rain. A glance around, and I saw most everyone else had already arrived and was seated at a large round table in the corner.

I headed that way, disappointed to find everyone but Tristan there. Great. Just what I wanted—a couples dinner where I was the one and only single person here. I forced myself to cast a bright smile around the group. "Hey everyone, how's it going?"

I slipped into one of two empty seats and draped my jacket over the back. Even though I had to bite my cheeks to keep from asking, I didn't ask where Tristan was. Fortunately, Liam was deep in the middle of a conversation with Alex and Ethan about something to do with a new player on the team. Zoe was seated to my side and caught my eyes.

"Team drama," she said with a slight smile. "How've you been?"

"Same, same. Haven't seen you at the gym since the other week."

She rolled her eyes. "I know. I've got this big finance case that's been tying me up. I'm spending way too much time at the office."

Ethan leaned our direction, dropping a kiss on her cheek. "Yes, you have." He caught my eyes. "Please tell her to stop working so hard. She won't listen to me," he said with a wink.

"Of course, I'll badger her for you," I offered with a grin.

At that moment, I felt Tristan's presence. That's how attuned to him I was. My back happened to be facing the entrance, so I couldn't see him approaching, but I literally felt his heat and strength come up behind me. A prickle of awareness ran up my spine, followed by a ripple of heat.

He slid into the chair beside me. I had to physically hold myself back from touching him. We'd gotten comfortable together now that we'd spent so much time with each other. I was used to easy touches, but I wasn't used to us being out in public like this, much less with our entire group of friends here as witnesses.

I managed a casual hello and was relieved Tristan was quickly drawn into the conversation about the team drama Zoe referenced. Our waitress arrived to take our order and serve drinks. The evening actually settled into a normal routine. I was almost comfortable enough to think about touching Tristan when I felt his palm slide over my thigh and give it a subtle squeeze.

My low belly clenched, and I was instantly wet. Okay, I wanted to act normal around our friends, but I didn't want to be squirming in my seat over wanting him.

I was saved for a most annoying reason.

"Oh hi Tristan," a female voice said brightly from behind us.

I glanced over my shoulder to see a stunning woman approaching the table with another equally beautiful woman beside her. I didn't spend much time thinking about my appearance. It was something I was mostly confident about. Oh, I wasn't all arrogant about it, but I knew I was no ugly duckling and was confident in my brain, so I could cast aside feminine doubts about my looks. There was one thing I got a little insecure about here and there though—my height and my pretty generous curves. I was on the short side, so every curve seemed even larger since there wasn't any room to stretch out.

Anyway, these two women were tall and willowy, quite the opposite of my short, curvy self. The one who'd greeted Tristan had a sharp, possessive air to her. One glance at her and the description I promptly assigned her was *shallow bitch*. I watched as he looked up. His eyes didn't give much away, but I saw a flicker of surprise followed by the narrowing of his gaze.

"Hi Renee," he said perfunctorily.

Fucking great. This was Renee. Just what I needed—the reminder that Tristan didn't dally with anyone and cut women out of his life with the precision of a scalpel if they expected too much. Renee flicked her long, blonde hair off of one shoulder and rested her hand on her hip. She was the epitome of stylish and gorgeous with her model thin figure, her straight blonde hair and blue eyes. She was dressed in silky black slacks with a fitted white blouse that cinched at her waist. Oh, how I wished I didn't know she'd recently been involved with Tristan.

At his rather flat reply, Renee arched a brow. Her friend stayed quiet, her eyes scanning the table. When Tristan let the silence stretch, Renee rolled her eyes. "Well then, I suppose it means nothing we saw each other for almost a year," she said with a snide tone.

Tristan's eyes darkened. Everyone at the table had gone quiet. If there was one thing I knew well about Tristan—he didn't do drama. He despised gossip and kept a remarkably low profile for an international sports star. The other thing I knew well about Tristan—he didn't do relationships, and he certainly didn't appreciate a spectacle. Renee publicly confronting him like this would not be something he appreciated. At all.

His eyes flicked between them, and he stood quickly. Moving smoothly, he slipped his hand through Renee's elbow and escorted her away from our table. Her friend followed along a few feet behind them. I couldn't keep from watching. Tristan stopped beside the entrance and stepped back. I could see him speaking. Whatever he said, Renee looked annoyed. When he walked back toward our table, she didn't follow and left the restaurant.

He sat down and drained his beer. When he looked up, all eyes were on him, although I was trying to be casual about it.

"What?" he asked.

"You're the one who never has to deal with drama. Can't help but wonder how you're doing," Ethan said with a shrug and a sly grin.

Tristan rolled his shoulders and shook his head with a sigh. "Right mate. I can do without it. Let's not make it more than it was."

Olivia's eyes caught mine from where she sat at an angle across from me. I could see the concern in her gaze. I knew she'd be worrying how I was interpreting that little interaction. She had good reason. Everything about it reminded me why I'd spent a year avoiding Tristan. Too late for a do-over on that though. I'd jumped in and was already over my head now. I swatted away the thread of insecurity that the tall and willowy Renee's presence had tugged loose inside. That and the way Tristan dismissed her. Because I knew he was an honest man, I knew he hadn't misrepresented what he wanted to her. He was so up front about the fact he wasn't interested in even entertaining the idea of a relationship that it was a known fact publicly and the very reason I'd tried to kill my desire for him with avoidance. I couldn't really think about any of this now. The last thing I wanted was for our friends to observe me feeling awkward.

Our waitress stopped by to check on us, and I had her fill my wineglass and bring another bottle for the table. The tension from Renee's appearance dissipated once conversation moved on. I could sense Tristan's tension, but I ignored it. I was feeling prickly and annoyed as much with myself as with him. I needed not to care so much, but I did.

I filled my wine glass again and took a slow sip, staying quiet, which wasn't like me. Not in a group of friends like this. The buzz of the wine softened the edges of my annoyance and helped me shove my insecurity far to the back of my mind. Somewhere in the midst of a good natured debate between Liam and Ethan, I felt Tristan's hand curl over my thigh again. I glanced his way reflexively, colliding with his hazel gaze. Sweet hell. He had amazing eyes—layers of green, gold and nutmeg—with thick dark lashes that curled against his cheeks. It was almost obscene for a man to have lashes like that, but then this was Tristan and he'd been ridiculously blessed when it came to looks.

"You okay?" he asked, his voice low.

My throat tightened with emotion. Great, just great. My defenses were down, and this was bad, really bad.

"Uh huh," I said with a rapid nod. "I'm good."

He searched my gaze, and I prayed he couldn't see how exposed I felt. His hand was a hot brand on my thigh. Butterflies amassed in my belly, and I could feel the slick heat in my core. No matter what, my body betrayed me when it came to Tristan. I didn't want to want him the way I did, but I was helpless to stop it.

He finally nodded, just barely. "Okay. Shall we go?"

My body almost started jumping up and down. *Yes! Let's go. The sooner we leave, the sooner we can get naked and you can be buried inside of me.*

Did I really just think that?

Yes, yes you did.

His hand gave a subtle squeeze, and I looked back to him, nodding before an actual thought could keep me from doing anything else.

I couldn't think past the need flooding my body in hot waves. I should be thinking about how to gracefully untangle myself from Tristan. Yet, it was becoming beyond obvious I was already in way too deep.

Between the desire thrumming through me and the wine fuzzing my thoughts, I didn't even notice Tristan already saying our goodbyes until he started to stand. My mind snapped to the moment, and I glanced around the table. No one seemed to notice anything amiss. Ethan was laughing at something, and Zoe was rolling her eyes at him.

I felt Tristan's hand curl over my shoulder. Reflexively, I reached up, and he laced his fingers with mine as he pulled my chair back. I stood and glanced around the table.

Olivia caught my eyes. "So we'll see you at the game tomorrow?" she asked, appearing to reference a conversation we'd already had.

"Of course!" I said, injecting a cheery tone into my reply.

"Perfect, Harper's driving, so we'll pick you up," she said matter-of factly.

Wow. My entire evening was planned out tomorrow and somehow I'd been so zoned out over Tristan, I'd nearly missed the fact I'd made plans.

"Sounds good. What time again?"

"Five. Good night," Harper added with a wave.

"I'll be ready," I said with a smile. I managed the rest of my goodbyes and headed out, my hand held in Tristan's warm grip.

I was so bad off, I even loved having him hold my hand. The fact he didn't try to hide it made my heart do a little dance.

Chapter Twenty-Three

TRISTAN

I held the door open at Daisy's place, and she walked through in front of me. I couldn't say why but we always stayed at her place. Well, perhaps I could say why. I liked it. My flat was perfectly fine, but it wasn't as warm and inviting as Daisy's. Everything about her place screamed Daisy with it's brightly colored rugs and throw pillows scattered on the couch. It was also warm and comfortable...as she was in ways that made it hard for me to think about.

I closed and locked the door behind us. It briefly crossed my mind that I was assuming I'd be spending the night here. I toed off my shoes and glanced across the room. She was walking through the archway into the kitchen, her hips swaying with each step. She must've come straight to dinner from the office because she had on her almost appropriate work clothes. Her black skirt landed just above her knees and otherwise hugged every inch of her luscious hips like a lover. She'd paired that with a quite appropriate white blouse, save the fact the buttons were strained by her generous breasts. She tossed her purse on the kitchen table and turned, kicking her shoes off as she did.

My cock had been hard for hours now. My only respite the entire evening had been when Renee showed up. One look at her, and the need pounding through me temporarily cooled. I'd been pissed, mostly because I hated the drama of it. I'd been nothing but completely upfront with Renee the entire time we'd occasionally seen each other. Hell, she was the one who'd put a stop to our arrangement once or twice when she was seeing other guys.

When I'd walked away from the table with her, she'd shifted gears and seemed embarrassed. As nicely as possible, I'd reminded her things with us were over. I felt bad about the whole thing, if only because I'd obviously missed the cues she was reading more into things than I was. I might have had crystal clear boundaries about expectations when it came to relationships, but I wasn't an ass about it. I never set out to hurt anyone. I don't know that Renee was overly hurt, as much as her pride had taken a hit. She was used to being chased and was stung that I wasn't giving her that little thrill.

The moment Renee left, my entire attention had swung back to Daisy. I'd had to sit through the torture of seeing the valley between her breasts all evening with her musky scent drifting up to me. I walked toward her, my eyes locked to hers. It felt as if the air between us was vibrating with the force of our desire. She leaned her shoulder against the inside of the archway and traced her fingertip along the V of her blouse.

Oh my fucking God. She was going to kill me. I'd come to learn Daisy wasn't the least bit shy when it came to sex. Pity for all the men before me who'd failed to satisfy her because they had no idea what they were missing. I stopped about a foot away, my cock so hard it ached. She flicked one button and then another and another, her blouse falling open. Behind her almost proper white blouse, she had a see through white lace bra on. It was close to pointless and doing a pathetic job of covering anything up.

Her dusky pink nipples peeked at me through the lace—taut and perky. My mouth watered to taste them, but I held back and waited. Daisy's hands hooked over the waist-band of her skirt and pushed it down slowly, shimmying her hips as she did. It fell around her feet. With a flick of her foot, she kicked it away. With a shake of her shoulders, her blouse slid down her arms and slid to the floor in a soft whoosh.

She now stood before me in nothing but a scrap of white lace panties and that ridicu-lous excuse of a bra. My control was frayed to the point of snapping, and I didn't even care. In two strides, I reached her, lifted her against me and walked straight back until we bumped the kitchen counter. With her legs twined around me, I didn't want to create any distance, but I needed enough space to get my cock out and bury it inside of her.

I eased her hips onto the counter and stepped back.

"Hey, where are you going?" she asked, biting her lip and narrowing her eyes.

"Nowhere," I managed as I caught my

shirt behind my neck and lifted it off, flinging it to the floor behind me.

I *needed* to feel her bare skin against mine.

I looked back to Daisy to see she'd propped her feet on the edge of the counter. Fuck me. I was close enough to see the wet silk between her thighs. Whether she meant it or not, she'd just put her pussy on display for me. I shoved my zipper down as I stepped to her, roughly dragging my fingers over that wet silk as I did. I pushed the silk out of the way with a groan and buried two fingers in her. She was drenched, her channel pulsing around me instantly.

I was distracted at the delicious feel of her and didn't notice she was busy pushing my jeans and briefs down. My cock bounced free, and she curled her palm around it.

I meant to drag this out, to make her as insane as I felt inside, but I simply couldn't. I didn't have the control and need was raging like a wildfire inside of me.

"Oooh," she murmured, sliding her thumb over the pre-cum at the head of my cock.

Dear God. She *was* going to kill me. She released me only to suck on her thumb, her eyes on me—those wide brown eyes that could bring me to my knees with a look.

She drew her thumb out with a pop, the sound mimicking the snap of my control inside. I slid my fingers out of her and yanked her to the edge of the counter. Gripping my cock in my fist, I positioned it at her entrance. Her pussy was pink and so wet it was glistening, and the insides of her thighs were damp.

A soft gasp came from her when I dragged the head of my cock back and forth in her folds. On the heels of her breath, I surged into her, sinking to the hilt at once. I looked up, colliding with her gaze. My heart clenched, a wave of emotion rocking me, mingling with the need burning like fire in my veins.

Her eyes were hazy and dark, her cheeks flushed pink. I held still, my heart thudding against my ribs. Lifting a hand, I brushed a loose lock of hair out of her eyes. On a breath, I began to move. Her legs curled around my hips, and she flexed into me with each thrust. Inside of seconds, I was pounding into her, holding onto her for dear life as pressure tightened inside of me. I could feel her channel start to throb around my cock and reached between us to swirl my thumb over her hot, wet button of need.

She cried out, my name falling in a

broken shout. Her core clenched tightly around my cock, sending my release hurtling through me. I distantly heard my own voice growling her name over and over. I was so spent from the force of my release, it was a damn good thing I could lean into the counter. Otherwise, I was fairly certain I'd have stumbled. My forehead fell to hers, and I curled my arms around her.

Her skin was damp against mine, and it suddenly occurred to me I hadn't even bothered to take time to taste her nipples. I could feel their taut peaks against me through the lace. I wasn't used to losing control the way I did with Daisy. A thread of unease ran through me, but I ignored it. It felt too good to be here—buried deep inside of her with her warm and pliant in my arms.

After a few minutes, her skin pebbled against mine, and I reluctantly lifted my head. I started to draw back, but she tightened her legs around me.

"Where are you going?" she murmured, a thread of a pout in her tone.

I looked back at her, fighting my grin. I gave in once she actually cocked her head to the side and pouted.

God, I loved this woman.

Whoa. What the bloody hell did I just think?

My mouth almost dropped open. I loved her? As my mind tested this question, the answer was resounding. Yes. I loved her. I remained still for a beat, trying to get ahold of myself. I was still balls deep inside of Daisy. The physical moment grounded me. I clung to that and ignored the rest for now.

"You're cold," I replied, stating the obvious.

"I know, and you're warm," she countered.

I couldn't help but laugh. I stepped back to her and lifted her against me. "In that case, I'll carry you to the shower."

She easily curled her legs around my waist and looped her arms around my shoulders as I carried her down the short hallway to her bedroom. A steamy shower reminded me that I was all but a slave to Daisy. Or rather my body was. I generally considered showering a practical task. With her beside me, soap bubbling on her skin and every inch of her lush body right there, well, it never felt too practical. More than once we'd run out of hot water.

A bit later, I stared up at the ceiling in the darkness. Because it was Daisy and she was ever whimsical, she'd decorated her ceiling with glow in the dark constellations. They glowed softly in her bedroom. I fell asleep thinking the end of our month was racing toward us, and I didn't know what the hell to do. The only comfort was to pull her close and savor the feel of her against me.

DAISY

I stared idly at the row of pasta boxes on the shelf in front of me. I was squeezing my grocery shopping in at lunch because tonight the Seattle Stars had a game. I might have a vivid recollection of the feel of Tristan buried inside of me last night, but I only vaguely recalled Harper and Olivia were picking me up for the game this evening. The haze I'd been floating along in was clouding my entire life. I couldn't remember to take care of the basics and hardly remembered plans I made with friends. My cabinets were bare enough I needed to get some groceries. Tristan's presence in my life was pushing everything else out of the way, and I wasn't so sure what to think about it. I was normally a fairly organized person, but I hadn't been shopping in over two weeks and only realized how bad the situation was when I went to grab a yogurt this morning, and there were none. That led to the discovery I was out of coffee, eggs and every other basic item I liked to have around.

So here I was shopping at lunch because I couldn't even contemplate not going to the game tonight. For one, I enjoyed watching the Stars play. I'd avoided going to games for too long once I started avoiding Tristan. Now, the idea of not seeing him tonight almost made me physically ache. Oh hell. I knew I was in deep, but every so often it hit me like a hammer to my heart. Another weekend, and we'd be at the end of our month. I occasionally allowed myself to obsess over what Tristan meant by 'reassess.' Most of the time though, the second I started thinking, anxiety bloomed in my chest.

Like right now, I kicked that train of thought to the curb and contemplated the fact that there were way too many choices of pasta. I snagged several different boxes, tossed them into my cart and kept moving. As I wheeled around the end of the aisle, I almost ran someone over and came to a quick stop.

"Sorry about that!" I exclaimed as I looked up.

Right into Renee's face. Renee whose last name I didn't know and who I really, *really* didn't want to care about. There she stood, looking pretty much perfect for a grocery store run. I mean, I looked good in my usual workday outfit of a blouse and fitted skirt with low heels. My hair was up in a twist, and I had on dangly silver earrings today to match my silver bracelets. I liked the way the earrings felt when I turned my head—playful and silly. Still though, I was busy and in a rush and instantly felt flustered.

Renee had to be close to six feet tall and looked down at me. I swear, she wrinkled her nose.

Shallow, petty bitch.

Really? You're going there? It's not like you don't know why she has a thing for Tristan.

Okay, fine. I'll cut her a little slack. But still, does she have to look so fucking perfect?

I sighed internally and straightened my shoulders, giving her a carefully polite smile. She flicked her hair over her shoulder and eyed me.

"So, you're Tristan's latest?" she asked.

Well, geez. I was all prepared to try to be nice, but she had to go and start there. Claws out. I could win an award for bitchiness when called upon.

I arched a brow. "Excuse me?"

Renee rolled her eyes. "Look, I'm not stupid. I saw the way he was looking at you. Let me just give you a little warning. If you haven't already figured it out, he's incredible in bed. Just don't let yourself hope for anything more. He's uptight as hell about 'expectations' and even when it's obvious there's more going on than he wants to admit, he'll act like there's not," she said, complete with a snide tone and air quotes.

There was no way in hell I'd let on that she managed to hit right at the core of what made my heart ache and my mind start running in circles over Tristan. Annoyed she'd managed to do that even though she didn't even know me, I felt hot and prickly and not in a good way.

"Sounds to me like jealousy talking. Tristan is nothing more than a friend. Maybe you should wise up and stop making a fool of yourself," I said, not even bothering to hide my snippy tone.

Renee's eyes widened and then narrowed before she let out a bitter laugh. "I suppose you have a point. Well, if you're just friends, I'd suggest keeping it that way."

At that, she stalked off, her heels striking the tiled floor loudly with each step she took. I stayed where I was for a beat, pointlessly slipping my phone out and reading my grocery list. My chest was tight, and my gut was churning. As pissed as I was that Renee had dared say anything, I was reeling from how accurately she'd zeroed in on my fears. Hope —stupid, feckless hope—kept trying to convince me Tristan felt something for me too. Perhaps he did. It didn't change the fact he was who he was, and he'd been nothing but clear about his limits.

Later that evening, I sat with Harper and Olivia in the owner's box at the stadium. It was halftime, and we'd just fetched drinks and were seated at a small table in the corner where we had a clear view for the game, but could relax and actually hear each other speak. I didn't mind the perks of being friends with enough team members and their respective spouses to be able to watch the games up here, but sometimes I missed the messiness of being in the crowd.

Tonight was one of those nights. I could've used the low cacophony and the buzz of the crowd to get my mind off of its treadmill of Tristan. I'd considered canceling, but I'd been torn. It was never easy to back out of group things, not when I had friends who knew me too well. Even worse, as off kilter as I'd been since running into Renee at the store, I couldn't seem to keep away from Tristan. I wanted to see him. Badly.

I took a sip of my wine and looked out over the stadium. Olivia was talking with someone I didn't recognize, while Harper was listening to a voice message on her phone. Another few minutes passed, and I must've zoned out until I felt a nudge on my shoulder. I turned to see Olivia grinning.

"What's on your mind?" she asked.

I shrugged. "Not much. Long day at work."

Olivia nodded slowly, a curl bouncing on her cheek. "So, things seem pretty, uh, hot and heavy with you and Tristan," she said, not bothering to build up to her point.

My cheeks got hot, and I rolled my eyes. "Hot and heavy? All we did was have dinner."

Harper set her phone down, her perceptive gaze flicking between us. She stayed quiet though and took a swallow of beer.

Olivia returned my eye roll. "Dinner while Tristan could barely keep his eyes off of you. I thought he was going to throw you over his shoulder and carry you out."

Harper bit her lip to keep from laughing. I glanced between them and sighed. "Is this how it's going to be? If you're wondering why I didn't want everyone to know about us, this would be the reason."

Olivia cocked her head to the side, the gleam in her eyes fading. "Okay, okay. I couldn't help it. I mean, he was so obvious about it, I couldn't believe it."

"I stand by what I said before. He likes you. A lot," Harper added.

Oh God. I did *not* need this. Hope—stupid, annoying hope—started practically spinning in circles inside my heart. A few years ago when I decided it was time to find the right guy, I'd been so hopeful and confident about it all. Because I was who I was, I'd told the whole free world about it. I'd been rather let down at first because all the men I came across seemed permanently stuck in college —they just wanted to have a little fun and move along. I'd gotten hopeful all over again when Olivia and Liam found each other. I'd thought that was how it was supposed to happen. Then, Harper and Alex collided and the magic happened all over again. I mean, hell, Harper had officially sworn off men after she'd been raped in college. She truly hadn't been looking for love, but it found her anyway.

All through that, I'd tried to stay hopeful, but my hope got tired and ragged around the edges, like an old, worn blanket that couldn't keep me warm anymore. I'd been stunned when Ethan fell for Zoe. My God, he was the player of all players—nothing but light and casual for him. Tristan might not be into serious relationships, but Ethan had taken it to another level altogether. Now, to look at him with Zoe, it was hard to believe he'd ever been like that. He flat out adored her and would do just about anything for her.

So there I was with my hope, which was just too tired to keep me trying much more. I'd figured that was part of the problem. I'd been trying too hard to find someone. Then, I kissed Tristan in that stairwell at the hotel, and it was like I couldn't let it go. Now, I'd gone and fallen for him. Hard. I'd spent most of the afternoon trying to shore myself up inside and remind myself no matter what happened with us, it was worth it to have the time I'd had with him. The sex was mind-blowingly good. He'd more than kept his promise to give me an orgasm. I'd had so many I'd lost count. I seriously doubted anyone else could meet the standard he set. I needed a reality check, preferably yesterday.

So I looked over at Harper and tried not to get too excited.

Olivia had to go and make things worse for me.

She looked to Harper and nodded emphatically. "You're right, but then you usually are."

Olivia looked back to me. "I've never seen Tristan the way he was last night. Because Liam makes me go to all the team stuff with him..."

"Oh you want to go," Harper added with a nudge of her elbow in Olivia's side.

Olivia flushed and shrugged. "Okay, maybe I do. Anyway, thing is because I've been to so many places with them, I've seen Tristan on other dates. I don't even know if he would call them a date, but whatever. Anyway, my point is, he's never looked at anyone the way he was looking at you. Honestly, I'd never say he was rude because he's not. Tristan is nothing but nice, but when it comes to women, I always thought he was a bit distant. Not with you though. Oh no." She fanned her face with a sly grin.

By this point, hope was stomping its feet and pounding its chest. I managed to laugh a little, but it didn't last. I wanted too much. Even worse, Tristan just had to go and be practically the perfect guy for me. Let's start with the obvious—international soccer star with a body to die for. It didn't hurt at all he was too handsome for his own good with his dark curls, hazel eyes, chiseled featured and a mouth made for sin. I'd thought his mouth was sexy before he'd buried it between my legs and sent me flying time and again. So, on the surface, he was probably a 10 plus.

He was also smart without being a cocky jerk about it. My God, he was a doctor and he'd pulled off this feat while he was playing professionally. Granted, he'd told me himself he figured he'd have to put off his residency until he got injured. His injury bought him time he wouldn't have otherwise had. So there was another thing—he was a hard worker. He easily chatted with me about work without his eyes glazing over from the boredom of it all.

I was beyond in too deep. I loved him.

Chapter Twenty-Five

TRISTAN

I scrubbed a towel over my face and chest as I walked from the showers toward my locker. We'd won tonight, but it had been a bruising win. My knee was holding up fine, and I'd scored one of our team's two goals for the night. The locker room was humming with the chatter of the team and staff. I ignored everyone and dressed quickly. I had one thought in mind—Daisy and how soon I could get to her.

I'd seen her briefly right after the game, and she'd seemed out of sorts. On the surface, she'd been normal—friendly and teasing. Yet, I'd sensed a guarded quality to her. I didn't like it.

Not much later, we walked out into the

night. I'd driven here for the express purpose of driving Daisy home. I'd known she'd caught a ride here with Harper and Olivia, and I fully intended to spend the night with her again, so I'd planned accordingly. As I'd predicted, Alex caught a ride with me here and was now leaving with Harper. Olivia was latched to Liam, which left me with Daisy. Precisely what I wanted.

The late spring night was cool and damp. The sky had cleared this afternoon before our game, although it had rained this morning. The air was washed clean from the rain. I reached for Daisy's hand, a sense of relief rolling through me when she easily laced her fingers into mine. I didn't know what the bloody hell I was doing.

I'd come to the conclusion I'd forget about the silly limit I'd set and we'd just keep on going. Yet, I felt unsettled about that. Before anything had ever gone further between us, I'd known what Daisy wanted. Hell, she'd spelled it out—an orgasm and a commitment.

Ever since my abrupt realization that I loved her, I wasn't quite sure what to do with it. I didn't want to end things. In fact, I couldn't fathom doing that. Yet, I was so unsettled, I wasn't ready to consider a commitment. I merely wanted to buy some time—

time that didn't include any separation from Daisy.

In short order, we were at her place, and she was getting me yet another glass of water. I couldn't drink enough after I played. I leaned back into the cushions on her couch with a sigh. Reflexively, I ran my hand over my knee. No swelling and no pain. I'd worried that ACL tear could've been career-ending for me. Yet, a good surgeon, a long recovery, and the strictest physical therapist in the universe seemed to have sent me back stronger than before. I'd take it.

Daisy returned and handed me the glass of water before setting an entire pitcher of water on the coffee table.

I looked from the pitcher to her and grinned. "I can get my own water, you know?"

She flashed a smile. "Oh, I know. I figure you must be tired. This way, neither one of us has to move."

She hooked her foot under her knee and went to grab the remote. Before she had a chance to turn the telly on, my mouth decided to up and say something I'd been thinking about all day.

"About that month?"

I might've been thinking about it, but my

mind would rather have waited. Oh well, oh hell.

She swung to me, her brown eyes carefully scanning my face. "What about it?" she finally asked.

That's what I got for letting my words get ahead of me. That's the effect Daisy had on me. I'd never in my life gotten ahead of myself when it came to a woman. It had never been a challenge either. That was why I preferred to steer clear of relationships and the potential emotional landmines they contained. No matter, I'd gone and stumbled into this, I had to clear it up fast.

"I think we shouldn't worry about it," I finally said, striving to keep my tone casual.

She couldn't hear the pounding of my heart and the subtle thread of uncertainty weaving its way through me. There were many things I'd experienced in life, but uncertainty was very rare. I didn't quite know what to do with it, so I opted to ignore it.

"What do you mean?" she asked.

Bloody hell. She was not going to let me gloss over this.

I'd keep trying anyway.

"Just that. Let's not worry about it."

Her wide brown eyes held mine. She was quiet, almost too quiet. After a moment, she bit her lip and bounced her foot up and down.

"I'm not so sure that's a good idea," she finally said.

My heart started pounding even harder, and my gut churned. I was shaking my head before I could think. I set my water down and straightened, reaching for her hands. They were cold in mine, and I wanted to wrap her close to me and never let go. But she had that guarded look in her eyes, and she was worrying her bottom lip. Usually I'd think that was hot. Hell, I thought pretty much everything she did was hot. Right now though, I wasn't thinking like that.

"It just means nothing changes. That's all. Why is that not a good idea?"

Her eyes slammed to mine. For a few beats, I could hardly breathe. Her gaze held such raw vulnerability and such a depth of emotion, it grabbed at me. She gave her head a shake, and it disappeared with that careful look replacing it. She finally stopped chewing on her lip. On the heels of a deep breath, she spoke.

"Because I think I probably want more than you do, and I need to not make this any worse than it already will be."

Like an idiot, words just kept tumbling out of my mouth.

"Worse?"

She started worrying her bottom lip again, a heavy sigh escaping when she paused at it. "Uh huh. Look, I knew what I was walking into when this started, but I know we want different things long term. I want a commitment. You don't. It's probably best if we don't take things any further."

At this point, I was fairly certain my heart might pound its way out of my chest. A sense of panic rose inside of me, an entirely unfamiliar feeling. In fact, I could only think of one other time I'd felt like this, and even then it hadn't been this bad. The day I'd injured my knee, I'd felt so helpless—as if my control had been ripped from me. The pain itself had been tolerable, something I could manage. What had created the spinning panic inside was feeling as if my plans had been torn out of my hands. All that had to do with was my career as a footballer.

Right here, right now with Daisy, I scrambled to gain a sense of control over the emotions barreling through me. Of all the things I'd considered, I hadn't considered this. I'd thought perhaps I'd still want her from a purely sexual standpoint. I'd been spot on about that. Hell, the more I had of her, the more I wanted her. The desire between us kept feeding its own fire, burning hotter and brighter with each passing day. That part was easy. Yet, I hadn't ever considered this raw need that went beyond all boundaries I'd kept in place around my heart. Truth was, those boundaries hadn't ever been a challenge to maintain. Daisy had slipped past them all without me even knowing. The idea she might walk away from what we had had my gut churning and my heart clenching.

I stared at her, trying to think of the right thing to say when I wasn't quite ready to blurt out the truth. I loved her. I just needed to buy some time to make sense of what that meant for us. For so long, I'd firmly believed I'd steer clear of attachments like this. I wasn't so foolish to think things couldn't get messy just because I loved her. Daisy was a bold, opinionated, emotional woman—messy was practically her middle name. None of it would be simple.

I must've stayed silent for too long because she tugged her hands free from mine and stood up quickly. Inside of a few seconds, she was pacing back in forth in front of the fireplace, her arms crossed tightly in front of her.

"This is exactly what I mean. I say anything even remotely hinting at what we both know and you go all quiet." She stopped pacing and turned to look at me, her eyes piercing mine across the coffee table between us. "I never misled you, and you were nothing but honest with me. You didn't promise me anything more than a month of orgasms." Her cheeks turned pink, and her eyes glittered. "You've kept your promise. I just..." She paused and swiped at a tear rolling down her cheek.

I didn't even realize I stood and moved toward her. By the time I did, I was brushing another teardrop away with my thumb, murmuring her name and pulling her into my arms. She ducked her head against my chest and took a shuddering breath.

I had no idea what to say. The ground under my feet felt so unfamiliar. I was used to being one step removed from this kind of emotion. After a few breaths, Daisy lifted her head, and my heart gave a resounding thump. Her doe eyes were wide and glistening. I'd have done just about anything she asked right then.

Her shoulders rose and fell with a deep breath, and she gave her head a little shake. "Well, I might be a mess, but I can't seem to tell you to leave," she finally said. "I should, you know?"

Relief hit me so hard, it was visceral. I caught the edge of my internal control and managed to reply. "You don't say?"

She shrugged, her teeth catching her bottom lip again. "There's what I should do and what I want to do. You gave me a month. I don't want to be shortchanged," she said with a sly grin.

The vulnerability was still lurking in her gaze, but I could sense she'd latched onto her bold side and was playing it like a shield. I knew we'd come up against this very issue again in short order, but perhaps for the first time in my life, I was content to sidestep something.

"I'd never do that," I murmured, sliding my palm down her spine and over the curve of her bottom. I savored the hitch in her breath when I pulled her against my cock, which was hard and aching inside of a second.

I might not be ready to relinquish my sanity to the intimacy shimmering around us, but I had no trouble succumbing to the need —a need quite specific to Daisy—that burned like wildfire in my veins.

Chapter Twenty-Six

DAISY

I snapped my mouth shut and stared at the man standing in front of me. Objectively speaking, he was handsome with his dark brown hair, eyes to match and a fit body. I was in one of the break rooms at my office. Our company was medium-sized and employed enough staff that I knew I hadn't met everyone here, but I didn't recall meeting this guy before.

He'd just asked me out to dinner, rather abruptly I might add. Thoughts tumbled through my mind. The quick answer was no. I'd spent close to three weeks straight tangled up with Tristan every night, including last night. Yet, I'd resolved absolutely nothing with my weak attempt to set some limits a few nights ago. He'd given me no clue as to what he might be feeling either. All I knew was he didn't want things to end. Meanwhile, I was in love with him, and he was emotionally unavailable.

I forced my attention back to the man in front of me. "Um, you surprised me. Have we met?"

Seriously, the guy had some looks going for him, but he'd forgotten to even introduce himself.

He laughed softly. "Ah, you must have forgotten we met a few weeks ago. I'm Dan Keller. I'm heading up our media project."

"Oh, I'm sorry. Now I remember. I'm Daisy Knight," I paused and laughed at myself. "I suppose you know my name. If you don't recall, I'm one of the lead researchers here."

He inclined his head slightly. "I recall both your name and what you do," he said with a slight smile.

He paused, which only made me feel a tad more self-conscious. As I was trying to figure out a graceful way to manage this, he spoke again.

"Didn't mean to throw you off guard there. I tend to be direct. I'd love to have dinner sometime. How about you let me know later on if you'd like to take me up on it?"

I was nodding before I could think. He winked and strolled away. I watched and wondered. I finished pouring my coffee and thought maybe the best thing for me would be to try seeing someone else. It would be a clean break from Tristan.

I returned to my office and tried to bury my brain in data, but my brain wasn't having it. Ever since my weak attempt to set a limit with Tristan, my mind had been running in circles. I didn't want to end anything with him. Ever. Merely considering it made it feel as if my heart had been sliced open. Which was the problem. Maybe he felt more for me. Maybe not. But he wasn't shifting gears in terms of what we were doing. Don't get me wrong, sex with Tristan indefinitely was incredibly hard to consider stopping. But the more we were tangled up physically, the closer I felt entangled emotionally. I loved him, and I had to take steps to protect my heart.

My mind kept flicking back to my brief interaction with Renee. She was so accurate in her assessment, it pained me to think about it. I was a smart woman, and I needed to act like it. If all I wanted were sex, this would be an easy decision. As phenomenal as the sex was, I wanted more. Much, much more.

It was Wednesday. Because I was having a hard time letting go of Tristan, I was counting the days to the end of this stupid month. One more day. Why the hell was I doing this?

I needed to stop letting my heart get dragged around by my traitorous body. I could find someone else like Tristan, but I wouldn't stand a chance if I kept letting this drag out. Abruptly, I snagged my phone off of my desk.

Let's make a clean break. Technically, we have one more day, but I'm calling it now. I won't avoid you, but from this point forward, we're back to friends. No benefits included. If this feels abrupt, it's because it's the only way I can do this. I'm in over my head, and I want far more than you ever will. You've given me more than I could've imagined. Please don't stop by. I need time to myself.

There was so much more I wanted to say. I had to literally force myself to put the phone down, so I didn't tell him I loved him. I laughed, a sad little laugh because it was ridiculous to think of telling the first man I'd fallen in love with via text. In a way, it mirrored so much of the chasm between what we wanted. Tristan wanted neat and tidy arrangements. I wanted love, arguments, make up sex, someone to hold me after a long day, someone to cheer me on when life was skidding sideways, and babies. Oh my, I wanted babies. I wanted forever.

My throat was tight, and I didn't realize I was crying until I felt the moisture on my cheeks. I grabbed a tissue and blew my nose. I took several deep breaths. I was miserable, but if anything, this reinforced why I had to move on.

I didn't know if Dan would be the guy to sweep me off my feet, but denial was an excellent coping skill for me. No sense in wallowing in how much I missed Tristan.

If that didn't tell you how ridiculously in love with him I was, I didn't know what would. All I'd done was send a text to end things. I already missed the hypothetical event of seeing him tonight when I didn't even really know if I would've seen him tonight. That's how undefined our relationship was. We'd spent three weeks of every night together and only rarely confirmed plans ahead.

I forced my mind off of him and spun in my chair, pulling up my email on my laptop. I searched for Dan's email address in our staff directory and shot him off an email, suggesting we grab a few drinks after work this Friday. I hesitated and almost asked about tonight, but that felt too soon for my sanity.

It was nothing much, but I needed to do something to remind myself I wasn't tethered to being in love with Tristan forever. I'd find someone else, no matter how long it took.

Chapter Twenty-Seven

TRISTAN

"Bloody hell!"

I tossed my phone on the bench in the locker room and quickly dragged a clean t-shirt over my head. I'd just finished showering after practice. Because I was that obsessed with Daisy, I'd reflexively grabbed my phone, intending to text her and let her know I'd be stopping by with dinner.

My heart was thudding against my ribs, and I felt sick again. I was angry and terrified at once. I should've known Daisy would keep thinking. I wanted her to just forget about rehashing everything with us and let it happen.

No, mate. You don't want to talk about it, and

you want her to go along with that. She wants more, and she's not accepting anything less.

This was a disaster, but not the disaster I'd been worried about. I needed to straighten it out right now. I tossed my towel in the hamper at the end of the row of lockers. Turning back, I looked up to see Ethan walking toward me. He slid onto the bench across from my locker and started to smile. Once he caught my eyes, the smile faded.

"Eh, what's up? You look, well, you look upset," he said.

I ran a hand through my damp hair and shrugged. "Nothing much."

I didn't want to dwell on this. I needed to get to Daisy's place as fast as humanly possible.

Ethan, being the mate he was, wasn't letting me bolt on him though. "Hey, what the hell? You forget your manners?" he asked, standing to walk quickly alongside of me as I strode out of the locker room and down the long stadium hallway.

"Leave it alone. I need to see Daisy," I muttered.

Ethan caught my arm when we reached the door. "Not like this, you don't," he said firmly. "I don't know what's going on, but something's not right. Aren't you the one who always tells me to cool it before I do anything stupid?"

I caught his eyes and knew I likely looked out of sorts. I was a mess. All this time, I'd figured I preferred to steer clear of relationships because I didn't want the messy emotional stuff to deal with from someone else. I was floored to realize *I* could get this mucked up inside. My brain was like static, and I couldn't think past anything other than getting to Daisy and telling her she couldn't do this.

Ethan didn't let go of my arm, and I finally took a breath, letting it out in a long sigh. "Fine. I'm waiting," I said with a roll of my eyes. "Shall I count to ten? Would that let you know I'd taken a bit to cool off?"

"Maybe you should let me know what the hell is going on," he countered.

I fished my phone out of my pocket and handed it to him after opening Daisy's last text.

He let go of my arm and read the message. When he looked back up at me, I wanted to fucking scream at what I saw there. I could tell he felt badly for me. That's how far I'd fallen. My best mate—once the player of all players—was looking at me as if I was in a sad state. I suppose I was, but I generally prided myself on being able to keep my shit together without much fuss.

When he didn't say anything, I got restless. "Well?"

He handed me the phone back and cocked his head to the side. "Well, unless you want to make this thing real, you'd best respect her request," he said slowly.

"What the hell do you mean—make this thing real? It is real," I said.

We stepped through the doors into a cool drizzle. Standing under the awning at the back entrance to the stadium, I glanced to Ethan. He caught my eyes and arched a brow.

"You know what I mean," he said.

That static was buzzing in my brain, making it hard to think straight. I eyed him and ran a hand through my hair.

"How is it not real? I mean, hell, we even went public with everyone," I muttered.

Ethan heaved a breath and shook his head slowly. "Mate, her text says it all. Sure, obviously you're doing the dirty dance plenty, but Daisy's never been anything but upfront about what she wants. She wants the whole deal. Making it real means actually committing to that."

I looked away from him, wishing I didn't feel like this was slipping beyond my control.

Hell, it was already out of my hands. I was knocked on my heels and scrambling to catch my balance. I bloody hated it. This was not the way I was accustomed to handling things in any area of my life, particularly anything involving a woman.

I ran a hand through my hair again and eyed Ethan. "I didn't break things off with her," I said, a rather inane point at the moment, but it's what came out.

Ethan eyed me for several beats. For all of his teasing, devil-may-care manner, he was a thoughtful guy. Ever since he'd settled down with Zoe, he'd become more grounded. To be forced into wanting advice from him about a woman made me feel rather foolish to say the least.

"Breaking things off with her isn't the point. Without even knowing what you've talked about with her, I know you. You've said for years that you didn't do relationships. I don't blame you a whit for that. Only difference between you and me before I met Zoe was I wasn't so uptight about it like you. Probably had more fun though," he said with a sly grin.

I was too frustrated to laugh, but I managed to roll my eyes. "Your point?"

Ethan returned my eye roll and leaned his

back against the building while the drizzle fell steadily just beyond the edge of the awning. "My point is she wants more than something wishy-washy. She said it right in her text."

I stared at him and forced myself to take a breath. I couldn't fucking believe what I was about to ask him, but I had to know. "How'd you know?"

"Know what?"

"That Zoe was the one for you."

Ethan eyed me for a beat, his perceptive gaze boring into me. "Mate, you helped talk some sense into me." When I didn't say anything, he sighed. "It crept up on me. You had the brains to point out it was obvious she meant more to me than anyone I'd ever been with. I suppose it really hit me when I tried to think about what life would be like without her. I didn't want that. At all. Made me bloody crazy. Dunno if it's that simple for everyone, but for me, that's what did it."

My heart was hammering inside my chest. Daisy telling me it was over was making me feel crazy. I wanted time—time to come to terms with what it all meant, time to... Fuck, I didn't know what I needed time for, but I bloody hated feeling out of control of a situation. Daisy had ripped the control away from me with her text.

"If you don't know what you want, either man up or let her go. You can't have it both ways. It's not fair to her. If you were hoping you could turn her into one of your tidy arrangements, you should've known that would never work. Not with Daisy. So, as I said, man up or let her go," Ethan said, his green gaze boring into mine.

Ethan was so often teasing that when he was making a serious point, it was impossible to ignore. I eyed him for a beat and nodded. "Right then, mate."

I looked out into the drizzle, my mind running laps around Daisy.

Ethan pushed off of the wall and came to stand beside me. "Need a ride?" he asked.

He knew me well enough to know when I was done with a conversation. I hadn't solved anything, but there wasn't much else to say unless I said it to Daisy. I glanced to the side. "Nah. I'll walk."

Ethan arched a brow. "You'll be right wet in a few minutes."

When he was my flat mate, we frequently walked together to and from practices. I still lived within fifteen minutes of the stadium, yet Ethan and Zoe had recently purchased a home beyond the downtown area of Seattle. Hence, Ethan drove to and from practice these days, while I only did so once in a while.

I looked out into the drizzle, which suited my mood perfectly. I glanced back at him and shook my head.

He shrugged. "Suit yourself. Call if you need to."

At that, he jogged to his car. I started walking. Thought I didn't mind getting wet, I'd underestimated the chill and hadn't even bothered with a rain jacket. Roughly halfway to my flat, I ducked into a pub I frequented with my mates on occasion. Damp and chilled, I slipped onto a stool at the bar. In short order, I had a beer in hand. The bartender tossed a clean bar towel my way as well. I wiped off my face and hair and leaned back, savoring the rich beer.

I scanned the room, my eyes eventually landing on a woman I'd seen for a bit last year. Valerie had been as cut and dry as me about sex. I tried to recall why we'd ended our rather convenient and not messy at all arrangement, but couldn't seem to dredge it up from my memory. It crossed my mind that there wasn't a single detail about Daisy I could even fathom forgetting. I gave my head a shake and took a long drag on my beer. When I looked back up, Valerie was weaving her way through the tables scattered about the pub toward me. I let my gaze travel over her. She was tall and quite beautiful with long dark hair and flashing dark eyes. She favored bold colors and wore a bright red skirt that swished with her steps, a fitted black t-shirt with a red scarf draped around her neck.

Intellectually, I knew we'd had great sex and that was it. Now, I looked at her now and felt nothing, not even a fleeting interest. She reached me and dropped a kiss on my cheek.

"Tristan, I haven't seen you in ages. How are you?" she asked as she stepped back.

If I were being honest, I'd tell her I was a bloody mess inside. But that wasn't how we were with each other. I might know her intimately, but only in the physical sense. She'd been just as content as I had to keep our connection entirely superficial. I hewed to that now.

"Aside from wet, I'm as well as can be expected. Yourself?"

She smiled, her gaze warm and tinged with flirtatiousness. "As well as can be expected. Are you alone tonight?"

This was a question of layers. It's what we asked each other via text whenever one or the other of us was looking to get laid. I tried, bloody hell, I tried to want Valerie. If I could want her, then perhaps I could convince myself I could somehow move beyond Daisy. Yet, there was nothing. Not even a spark. Even trying to conjure one felt like a betrayal. I silently shook my head. Daisy had fucking dumped me via text, and I was worried about betraying her.

You're not playing fair, mate. She can't dump you when you haven't even said aloud that there's more going on than fucking her until you're both so lost in it you can hardly see past it.

That was my rational side, the side that had kept me from stumbling into the emotional quagmire in which I currently found myself. That same side knew quite well what I was facing.

I must've been quiet a beat too long because Valerie placed a hand on my shoulder and slide it down. The touch was teasing and testing. I felt nothing. I eyed her.

"I'm alone tonight, but I intend to keep it that way," I finally said.

I idly twirled my almost empty bottle of beer in my fingers on the bar, considering what to say next. Fuck it. I was curious about something.

"Mind if I ask you a question?"

Valerie smiled and brushed her hair off one shoulder, her motions graceful. "Of course not. Ask away?'

I leaned an elbow on the bar. "This might offend you, but can you remind me why we stopped seeing each other?"

Valerie threw her head back with a laugh. I objectively admired the graceful arch of her neck. Still nothing, not even a spark of desire. My cock, which Daisy appeared to own now, lay flaccid in my briefs.

Valerie's laugh petered out, and she looked directly at me with a rueful smile. "I'm not offended. I mean, perhaps I should be, but we weren't serious, and I liked it that way." She paused, her gaze turning thoughtful. "I don't know that we even talked about it. You texted a few times, and I told you I was busy. Then you stopped texting. Because I was busy. I fancied myself in love. I've since discovered that what we had was glorious because it was entirely uncomplicated. I wouldn't mind trying it again."

Ah, so it hadn't been anything specific that I knew of. I wasn't such an arse that I'd forgotten an important detail. I chuckled softly and nodded. "I suppose it was entirely uncomplicated, eh?"

Valerie flashed a smile. "It was." She

paused and angled her head to the side, eying me thoughtfully. "Mind if *I* ask *you* a question?" she asked, mimicking my earlier inquiry.

"It's only fair," I replied.

"Are you involved with someone? Seriously, I mean."

Bloody hell. Was I that fucking obvious?

Whatever. I didn't have anything to hide. She'd know something was afoot for the simple fact I wouldn't be taking her up on her request to restart our 'entirely uncomplicated' arrangement.

"I'm sorting out the answer to that one as we speak," I finally said.

Valerie's eyes widened and then she nodded slowly. "Well, I must admit I never thought I'd see the day Tristan Wells fell for anyone." She paused, her gaze scanning my face. "You love her," she said wonderingly. "Wow."

Oh fuck. Really? How in the hell could she tell I loved anyone just from looking at me?

"I think you might be taking things a bit far," I countered.

I needed to regain some semblance of control internally, so I latched onto denial. It might not be the wisest choice, but it could be quite effective. If I could convince someone else, perhaps I could convince myself all was not lost.

Valerie merely smiled. "Oh Tristan. You know, this is good. If *you* are even wondering about it, you love her. That's not what we had, but you're a good man. I always thought you'd make a great husband."

Her comment shocked me so much, my mouth dropped open. "Are you telling me...?"

She laughed and shook her head sharply. "I'm not implying I moped about wishing you loved me. We were in the same place at the same time emotionally. I didn't want attachments and neither did you. It was neat and tidy and simple. I could enjoy what you had to offer without wanting more. But I also knew there was more to you than that. Trust me, as a woman who wasn't looking for more, I had my fill of assholes who were total jerks about it. I remember thinking if you ever fell for someone, she'd be a lucky woman. I never hoped it would be me. We didn't and still don't have that kind of spark. Hell..." She paused and shrugged with a rueful smile. "...I might've extended myself to see what I might get, but I'm not stupid. There's nothing there between us anymore. I might as well be your sister. Anyway, my point is, let yourself enjoy it. She must be an amazing woman if she brought you to heel," she said with a wry grin.

I stared at her, trying to wrap my brain around everything she'd just said. I opened my mouth to reply, but didn't know what I meant to say, so I shut it again and finished off my beer. After a moment, I looked back to Valerie. "Right then. Never knew I was so obvious."

She smiled softly and placed her hand on my arm, giving it a gentle squeeze. "I bet this is driving you crazy. You do like to call the shots. Well, love doesn't always let you do that. Do right by her, okay?"

At that, Valerie dropped another quick kiss on my cheek and spun away, waving her fingers over her shoulder. I watched her stride across the room, once again actively trying to dredge up a physical reaction to her. Nothing. In fact, trying to think about desire made me think about Daisy.

I was so fucked.

Not much later, I stepped into my flat and closed the door behind me. The drizzle had picked up its pace to rain on the short walk from the pub. The sound of water dripping on the tiles in the entry way was loud in the empty, quiet flat. I flicked a light on and kicked my shoes off. I dragged my wet t-shirt off and shoved my jeans down, tossing everything into the hamper in the bathroom. I took a quick hot shower to steam away the chill and changed into dry clothes. Normally, I enjoyed quiet. Right now, my flat felt cavernous. I hadn't spent a night here in weeks.

I flung my refrigerator open to find next to nothing in there. I slammed it shut and snagged my phone off the counter, quickly making a call for pizza delivery. I stood in the center of my living room. As it was, my flat felt almost unlived in. The space had an expansive living room and kitchen with tall windows that faced the street and hardwood floors. The furnishings were basic with a black sectional couch, a coffee table and a flat-screen television mounted on the back wall. The kitchen was to the side with a counter for seating. I had two bedrooms, which I didn't need. I hadn't bothered to move after Ethan moved out to stay with Zoe.

Right about now, the space felt empty and bordering on lonely. I missed Daisy acutely. I would've told you before that I loathed messiness. My flat was always tidy. It wasn't too hard to keep it that way living on my own. I was either studying, at practice, or working during those long months when I was recovering from my knee injury. My mind spun to the way it felt to be with Daisy. She wasn't exactly a tidy person. Oh, she wasn't a slob, but her place was warm, inviting and lived in. She left things here and there. Splashes of color brightened the space.

Just thinking of it made my flat look straight out of a black and white movie—stark and bare, devoid of the bright, whimsical touch Daisy imprinted everywhere. Between Ethan's blunt talk and Valerie declaring I must be in love, I was over it. Every time I tried to think about life without Daisy, it felt gray and colorless and so lonely it ached. I grabbed my phone.

Chapter Twenty-Eight

DAISY

I reached for my phone and tapped the screen, rereading Tristan's text for perhaps the thousandth time since he'd sent it late the other night.

I need to see you. Please.

That's it. That's all he said. I'd first read it around two in the morning. I'd fallen asleep restless and out of sorts. I'd woken in the midst of a heated dream—a rather amazing sex dream involving Tristan, of course. I'd been so close to orgasm, I'd almost texted him back right then and asked him to come over. But then I'd read his message again. And again and again. It was the very definition of vague. The only clarity was I knew he wanted to talk. My heart was so hungry and my hope was so greedy, I was interpreting all kinds of things.

I tossed my phone back on my desk and put my face in my hands. Tears pressed hot against the back of my eyes. Last night had been awful. I'd missed him so, so much. The strength I'd scrabbled together to send him that text had worn thin by the time I arrived home. Dinner alone and a failed attempt to zone out watching a sci-fi flick had only made me miss him more. All the things I did that I usually enjoyed felt flat and pointless. It had taken an enormous amount of will not to call him and tell him I'd changed my mind. The only thing that kept me from doing it was the fact I was an emotional mess—exactly what I needed to get past. I'd only be delaying the pain if I kept putting it off.

If I gave in and went to talk to him, I could imagine where it would go. Just being near him would make me weak, and I wouldn't be able to hold my ground. Unless he was going all in on us, I needed to create some distance and get past the really hard part. The part where I physically ached for him, the part where my chest felt split open and my heart felt raw, the part where the desire I'd built up for him was like trying to come off of a drug. I'd never actually experienced addiction, but I'd seen it and knew what it was like to witness someone physically craving something so profoundly, they lost their sense of themselves and everything in them leaned toward their drug of choice.

Tristan had become mine. I had to end this, and end it fast, or I'd fall deeper into the madness.

I gulped in air, swallowing through the tightness in my throat. My breath filtered through my fingers when I let out a slow, controlled sigh. After another few breaths, I lifted my head and spun in my chair. I needed to work. Restless, I stood and walked quickly out of my office to the break room. I needed more coffee and needed to move. I was walking so quickly, I rounded the corner and ran right into Dan Keller.

"Oh! I'm so sorry!" I exclaimed, taking a quick step back.

His hand curled around my upper arm, steadying me before he dropped it. "You okay?" he asked.

I looked back at him. Dan with his dark brown hair and eyes. Dan who I thought I should feel a spark with, but didn't. Dan who had asked me out to dinner. I'd completely forgotten I'd emailed him about grabbing drinks after work.

I latched onto that as if it would save me from drowning. It wasn't a date. I wasn't ready for that. But it would be good for me to do something, to remind myself my heart wouldn't be tethered forever to Tristan.

I forced a smile. "I'm fine, just walking too fast. Nothing new there," I said with a shrug.

Dan slipped his hands in his pockets and nodded. I stood there, the smile pasted on my face feeling brittle, but I refused to let it disappear. I'd fake it until I made it through to the other side of this emotional quagmire. I wanted to blame Tristan, but I couldn't. I'd walked in with my eyes wide open. I needed to walk out with as much boldness.

I took a deep breath. "So how about we grab some drinks after work today?" I asked, injecting a casual, cheery note in my voice.

This was no big deal. Having drinks with someone from work was perfectly normal.

"Sounds good to me," he replied, his tone light. He'd previously responded to my email with a similar affirmative.

I managed another bright smile. "Excellent." I made a show of glancing at the clock on the wall at the end of the hallway. "How about we meet at Harry's at five-thirty?" I asked, referencing a bar one block away and a place often frequented by any number of employees here due to its proximity.

As soon as Dan started to nod, I smiled even bigger—it felt practically maniacal at this point—and brushed past him. "Okay then. See you there," I said quickly as I almost ran into the break room.

I didn't even hear Dan's reply and was downright relieved he didn't follow me in here. What the hell was wrong with me? It was no big deal to share a few drinks with a co-worker. I shouldn't be so freaked out about it.

Yeah, but he did actually ask you out. So it's kinda like a date.

It's not a date. It's just drinks after work.

Oh my God. You're being ridiculous. You're freaking out because he probably thinks it's a date. You don't want to date anyone. You want Tristan.

Ridiculous didn't quite capture my state of mind. I was literally arguing with myself. My hand shook as I attempted to pour coffee. Emotion rocked me again. I set my mug down, slowly put the coffee pot back on the burner and leaned my hips against the counter. I couldn't get my shit together.

Exactly why it was a good thing I'd called things off with Tristan. When I'd sent that stupid text, I'd had it in my head we'd somehow manage to be friends again. The idea of seeing him and facing the truth—that he didn't love me and never would—was like a knife slicing across my heart in thousands of tiny cuts. Each time I saw him, more cuts would accumulate.

I took several deep breaths, trying to gather myself. I was in the fucking break room, for God's sake. I could *not* fall apart here.

———

I sat at a round table tucked in the corner at Harry's Pub, my eyes scanning the room. It was a basic pub with a polished wooden bar and tables to match. Televisions were mounted in the corners and behind the bar, all of them displaying some sports game. There was a grouping of pool tables in the back, and a cluster of tables where I was. I'd ordered a pomegranate martini, mostly because I'd been so surprised to see it on the drink specials list.

The waiter had drolly explained they were trying a few new things. Seeing as Harry's was almost always busy and clearly did quite well with beer and basic pub fare, I found it amusing. That said, I was happy for the delicious drink. I needed something strong to settle my nerves. I was a few gulps into my drink when Dan came striding across the bar toward me. He flashed me a smile and raised his hand, signaling the waiter, as he slipped into the chair across from me. He ordered a beer and turned his attention to me.

"Didn't mean to be late. I got caught in a meeting with Dr. Hall's team," he explained.

"I didn't even notice. While I adore Dr. Hall, he's notorious for having meetings run over. He loves the minutiae. ."

Dan chuckled, his dark brown eyes twinkling. "I've noticed that."

He paused when the waiter arrived and delivered his beer. "So, here we are having drinks," he said, lifting his beer in a mock toast.

I decided to take him literally and clinked my glass against his beer before draining it and promptly waving for the waiter to bring me another.

I looked back to Dan and thought again that if it weren't for Tristan, I'd probably like Dan. I should. I mean, he was handsome and he seemed quite nice. He didn't have that casual, friends with benefits vibe that Bradley did. He had a good job and he even had manners. By all accounts, I should be interested.

Beyond a friendly interest, I felt nothing. My body didn't even kind of hum. I instantly realized I might be returning to a life of sex that bored me to tears.

I swatted away those thoughts. I needed to give anything a shot. The longer I stayed hung up on Tristan, well, the longer I'd be hung up on Tristan.

"That we are," I finally replied. "So tell me what brought you to our company?"

Thus began a rather predictable conversation where we told each other things about ourselves and showed a friendly curiosity about each other. Not too far into this exercise in futility, a prickle of awareness ran up my spine. Before I finished lifting my head to look toward the entrance, I knew it was Tristan.

That's how powerful of an effect he had on me. All he had to do was get somewhere near me, and a tidal wave of need rolled through me. I was caught in the riptide in a matter of seconds.

It must've started raining since I'd walked in here roughly a half hour ago. Tristan's dark hair was damp. Across the room, our eyes snapped to each other like magnets. Heat coiled low in my belly, and electricity sizzled through the air, as if a live wire was suspended between us. My breath caught, and I swallowed against the emotion rioting inside of me.

I completely forgot Dan was there until he glanced over his shoulder, the motion nudging me out of my trance. He looked to Tristan and back to me.

"I take it you know him," Dan said, his tone curious.

I managed to tear my eyes from Tristan's and look to Dan. I nodded, but for the life of me I couldn't think of what to say. My heart hammered away, and I could barely catch my breath. I was halfway through my third martini and promptly gulped the rest. The liquid courage I'd been coasting on tonight suddenly felt insubstantial. It was pathetic I needed courage just to get through drinks with someone.

Dan was quiet and took a slow pull on his beer. When he set it down, his eyes met mine thoughtfully. "Can I make an observation?"

I shrugged, feeling foolish and uncomfortable and painfully aware of Tristan's presence as he walked toward the bar. My eyes kept flicking to him, hungry to see him. He wore nothing other than a t-shirt and jeans. His t-shirt was damp and outlined his obscenely muscled chest and back. I was so bad off that the sight of the corded muscles in his back flexing as his arms swung made my mouth water. Desire—so absent with Dan—flared inside. It was as if I was a bell, and Tristan was the only one who could ring me. The sound echoed through my body in vibrations of need. Heat flooded my belly and limbs. All of this, and I was at a table across the room pining—literally pining—for Tristan while I sat across from another man.

Oh, having drinks with Dan was nothing bad per se. We'd barely gotten past the pleasantries, but it felt so awkward and wrong. It cheapened everything I felt for Tristan.

"I might as well," Dan said, his voice cutting through the haze of need clouding my mind.

"Might as well what?" I asked, finally looking back at him.

He laughed softly. "I have no idea who that is, but obviously he means something to you. I had enough sense to pick up you weren't looking for anything more than friendship. I don't know what's between you and him, but I think you should probably go talk to him."

I was so startled, my mouth dropped open. I quickly snapped it shut and started to shake my head. "No, no, It's just..."

Dan shrugged. "We can still be friends. I'm the kind of friend that tells someone when they're being foolish. Realizing that I have no idea what's gone on with you two, all I have to do is look at you, and I can see there's something there. Go talk to him."

Dan was so downright sensible and nice, I burst into tears. I needed sensible and nice. I didn't need the crazy tornado of emotion and need Tristan elicited.

Because he was a nice guy, Dan snagged a napkin from the table and handed it to me. He gave my hand a squeeze when I curled the napkin into my fingers. At that second, I sensed Tristan's gaze on me. He stood beside the bar, his hand gripping its edge. His eyes were dark. Roughly twenty feet separated us, and I could feel his anger so thoroughly, I felt as if I'd been punched in the gut. I tore my eyes from his and scrubbed the napkin Dan had handed me over my wet cheeks.

I looked up to see Tristan gulping a beer, his back to me. The urge to go to him was so strong, I had to grip my chair to keep myself in place.

"Daisy."

Dan's voice brought my focus back to him.

"What?"

"Just go talk to him. You obviously want to," he said.

"But I told you we'd have drinks and I don't know..."

"I've had a beer, and you've been making quick work of those martinis," he said with a quick grin. "I'm getting an idea why. Look, we can get drinks another time, but you've got something to deal with, so go do it."

When I didn't move, he cocked his head to the side. "Okay, lecture time. You don't know me well, but once upon a time I blew up something really good. I know the look in your eyes, so don't be stupid like I was."

He jammed his thumb in the direction of the bar. With my heart drumming so hard, it propelled me forward, I finally moved. I stood and meant to walk over to Tristan, but I just couldn't. I was too overwrought and anxious. Instead, I impulsively dashed out into the rain. I had no jacket and my purse bounced against my hip as I skipped around puddles. It had been overcast earlier and was full on raining now.

Suddenly, a large hand caught my arm. I stumbled slightly and spun around to find Tristan behind me. My breath was heaving, and I was drenched. My skirt had ridden up my thighs, the fitted cotton sticking to my skin. I was chilled through, but so hot inside it barely registered.

"Tristan."

For a beat, we just stood there, staring at each other.

The tears that had been pressing against my eyelids rolled down my cheeks, mingling with the rain. My heart was racing and emotions tore through me—joy, sorrow, confusion, and more. I'd missed him so, and it had only been three days since I'd seen him. Those days had felt like eons longer. His absence felt like the serrated edge of a knife being dragged across my heart again and again.

His hazel gaze bored into me, so intense I couldn't look away.

He opened his mouth as if to speak and then snapped it shut.

He leaned his head back and looked up into the rain for a moment before leveling his piercing gaze with mine again.

"I almost kicked that guy's ass," he said, his tone wondering as if he couldn't believe what he was saying.

"That wasn't a date," I said quickly. "I was just grabbing some drinks after work. Dan told me I should come talk to you, so here I am." I rubbed my hand over my heart as if I could soothe the ache.

Tristan reeled me closer to him, shaking his head slightly. "I figured I had two options—kick his ass or tell you how I feel."

My breath caught and my heart started pounding so hard, I could barely think.

"How about a lifetime of orgasms?"

"Just orgasms?" I countered, hope flying wild and free inside.

He shook his head. "No, a commitment too."

His shoulders rose and fell with a deep breath. "I love you, you know."

Words started spilling out of me. So many feelings were all bundled up. It was as if they'd been shoved into a closet. His presence opened the door, and everything tumbled out on the floor in a mess.

"I don't know what I was thinking when I sent that text, but I miss you and I don't like it. Not at all. I love you, and I didn't mean to be so stupid about it. I didn't..." Suddenly, it hit me. He'd just told me he loved me, and I'd barely absorbed it. My hand flew to my mouth. "You love me?"

The rain kept falling, and shivers ran through me. I paused to catch my breath.

Tristan stepped to me, pulling me flush against him, his mouth curling at one corner.

"That's what I said. I got worried you didn't even notice," he said, his low chuckle rumbling through me.

One hand slid down and cupped my bottom. I could feel the ridge of his arousal nestled in the cradle of my hips. He lifted his free hand and traced my lips. He hadn't said a word. I opened my mouth to say something only to have his lips slam to mine. Inside of a millisecond, his tongue was sweeping deep inside, tangling with mine. I plastered myself to him in the rain, the heat burning between us making me forget I was cold and wet.

Chapter Twenty-Nine

TRISTAN

Daisy moaned into my mouth and flexed against me. It felt so fucking good to have her in my arms. She was all curves. The scent of her encircled me—a hint of honey and a tinge of musk mingling with the rain. Water splashed against the back of my legs when a car passed us by. I broke free from her lips, but I couldn't keep from tasting her, kissing and licking my way along her jawline and down her neck. She gasped my name, and I drew back, just far enough to look in her eyes.

It was close to dark. The reflection from the lights of passing cars caught in her wet blonde hair. Drops of rain glittered on her eyelashes, framing her wide brown eyes. My heart drummed hard and fast. My throat tightened with emotion at the look of raw vulnerability in her eyes. Thoughts spun through my mind. I'd been walking past Harry's Pub on the way home and ducked in to escape the rain and perhaps numb myself with a few beers. I'd reasoned myself to a place of sanity about Daisy and planned to track her down and make her listen to me. I loved her, and I wasn't running from it anymore. I'd looked straight across the room and seen Daisy. Having drinks with another fucking man. I'd never experienced the kind of jealousy I had in that moment.

Then, he'd gone and reached for her hand when she looked upset. As I'd stood there contemplating whether to march over there and clock him, Daisy had dashed out of the bar. Daisy's response to me lowering myself to beg to see her had been met with complete silence. I'd tried stopping by her place to no answer. I missed her so much, it felt as if my chest had been carved open.

Now here she was, shivering against me, her eyes locked to mine. She said she loved me and the only way I could reply was to pour everything I felt into a kiss. Rain fell around us, drops rolling down her cheeks. I brushed a damp lock of hair off of her forehead and soaked in the sight and feel of her.

"I missed you," I murmured, my voice coming out gruff.

She pressed herself a little closer to me, a sound coming from her throat.

God, I loved her. So fucking much. I supposed perhaps I should let her know that rather pertinent fact again.

"I love you," I finally said, the words coming out quite easily for the second time. I'd been so afraid to say them. Yet right here, right now with her in my arms where she belonged, it wasn't hard. Not at all.

Her eyes widened and then she burst into tears. She buried her face in my chest and burrowed closer, shudders running through her.

I had no practice with this, so I just held on, sliding my hand in sweeping passes up and down her back and tucking my head into her neck. I breathed her in. I have no idea how much time passed before her shudders stopped and her breathing evened out. She lifted her head and pressed her forehead to mine when I met her gaze.

"You could've said something sooner," she said.

I chuckled. "Ah, well luv, I didn't quite

sort it all out until a few days ago. I forgot how thoroughly you could avoid me."

She bit her lip, a small smile curling at the corners of her mouth.

"Well, your text was a bit vague."

"I said please."

She laughed a little then, sniffling and dragging her sleeve across her nose. Her gaze sobered. "That really wasn't a date. I don't want you to think..."

"Oh I thought all kinds of things. It's a good thing you ran out, or I probably would've clocked him. Instead, I had to chase after you."

The jealousy had faded, but I'd be damned if I'd let that happen again.

She chewed on her lip. "I was trying to tell myself I could get over you, but Dan might as well be my brother. I mean, I don't have a brother, but you should thank Dan. He told me it was obvious you were important to me and not to be stupid."

"Ah, did he now?"

She nodded fervently, her forehead bumping mine.

"Maybe when I'm not so bloody jealous of him, I'll thank him. I might need a few days to recover."

She bit her lip and sighed. Just that—the

sight of her teeth denting her plump bottom lip—and need shot through me so hard, my knees almost buckled. I trailed my fingertip along her jaw to trace her lips. They were warm in contrast to the cool rain on her skin. Her tongue darted out, and she drew my finger into her mouth. The subtle suction got me so hard, I could barely breathe for it.

Lust pounded through me. All I knew was I needed her. *Now.* I reluctantly dragged my finger out of her mouth and glanced around, my eyes landing on a set of stairs that disappeared around a corner. We weren't in the busiest part of downtown Seattle, and it was a rainy evening with rush hour winding down. All I wanted was enough privacy to slake the need driving me so hard I could hardly think.

Keeping her tight against my side, I all but dragged her up the stairs and around the corner to find a small entryway leading to another set of stairs between two buildings. I surmised the stairs led to flats above the businesses, but all I cared about was that we were out of sight and marginally protected from the rain by the slight overhang.

Spinning Daisy's back to the wall, I lifted her against me and fit my mouth over hers. I thanked all that was holy she didn't hesitate.

Her mouth was as greedy as mine with her tongue tangling wildly as she gasped and moaned while she shoved at my wet t-shirt. Her hands were chilly against my skin, but I was on fire so the contrast only amped up the heat.

My cock was so hard, the pressure was close to unbearable. Her nipples were tight little points pressing against me. I drew back because I needed to see her. I glanced down to see her nipples straining against her thin, cotton blouse. I rolled one between my fingers as I adjusted her in my arms, shoving her skirt up her legs. She didn't hesitate and wrapped her legs around my waist.

With the sound of the traffic passing us by, unseen from where we were tucked away, and rain pattering on the concrete landing where we stood, I shoved her panties out of the way and dragged my fingers through her folds. She was hot and wet. I sank a finger inside of her, knuckle deep, and almost came at the feel of her clenching around me.

"Tristan..." she murmured, her voice trailing off on a gasp when I added a second finger, stretching and stroking into her channel.

"Hmm, luv?"

Another gasp, and her legs tightened around me.

"I need you inside. I can't..."

Her head fell against the side of the building. I could hardly bear to take my fingers out of her, but my need to have my cock buried deep inside of her trumped my wish to keep teasing her. Holding her with one hand and capturing her lips in another bruising kiss, I shoved my zipper down and pushed my briefs out of the way, gripping my cock in my fist. I tore my lips free from hers only so I could look in her eyes when I sank inside of her.

I held still for a beat.

"Daisy."

I barely managed to speak, her name coming out in a choked whisper.

Her eyes opened, her liquid brown gaze slammed to mine. I swallowed, my heart clenching tight. On the heels of a breath, I slid into her in one swift surge. Her breath came out in a low moan, her lids dropped, but she didn't look away.

"I meant what I said," I murmured as I drew back and sank into her creamy clench again.

"What... Oh Tristan," she moaned.

Bloody hell. The sound of her saying my

name in that husky voice nearly made me come right there. I hung onto the thinnest thread of control.

She felt so good, slick, wet and pulsing around me. I forgot I'd meant to say something until she spoke again.

"What did you mean?"

"I love you."

My heart felt as if it might fly out of my chest—the enormity of my feelings for her and the relief at finally letting go of fighting them was almost too much to contain. But Daisy was here with me, held tight against me, and it would be okay.

Her eyes teared up again. Next thing I knew she was murmuring she loved me, and I was futilely wiping tears mingled with rain off of her cheeks. At some point, she laughed softly and tightened her legs around me, shifting her hips just enough to remind me I needed her more than I needed air to breathe, or at least that much.

I drew back again, savoring the feel of her wet heat caressing my cock. In a matter of seconds, my release was thundering through me. I reached between us, pressing my thumb against her hot little button of need. Her channel throbbed around me, and she cried out just as pleasure lashed at me, so hard I had to catch my balance on the wall behind her. With my breath heaving, I spent myself inside of her. She held on tight, and I savored the feel of her heart pounding against me.

I adjusted her in my arms, sliding my hand along her thigh. At the feel of her pebbled skin under my palm, awareness broke through the haze of need and emotion clouding my brain. I lifted my head and looked around. We were barely out of view of the sidewalk. Now that I wasn't driven entirely by need, I could see that perhaps we weren't in the best spot. Inside of a second, anyone could come up the steps behind us and turn to find us here.

I caught her lips in a quick kiss and started to draw back. She tightened her legs around me.

"Where are you going?" she asked, a mutinous look in her eyes.

"Luv, it's raining, we're both wet and any minute now we might run out of luck and give someone an accidental show."

Her eyes widened, and for a moment, I savored the fact she appeared to have completely forgotten where we were as well. She bit her lip and nodded.

"Oh right."

I eased away, quickly tucking myself back into my jeans and helped her pull her skirt down. I paused and glanced down at her. "Did you drive or walk?"

"Oh, I drove! Let's go to my office and then home."

My heart gave a hard thump as I curled my hand into hers. We walked through the rain together. In short order, we were back at her place. She was visibly shivering and had been ever since we got to her car. I tugged her into the shower. Not much later, she was curled up beside me in bed. I stared at the glow in the dark stars on her ceiling and considered that I finally felt like I was home. Home wasn't a place. Home was Daisy.

Two years later

"Shut the fu..." I slapped my hand over my mouth, looking over to see Tristan's shoulders shaking.

"Please be quiet," I said, rephrasing with a syrupy sweet voice and glaring at him.

We were at the kitchen table, and our one-year old daughter, Lily, was busy chasing cereal around on her high chair tray. Tristan had just informed me we needed more diapers because he'd apparently forgotten to get them from the store yesterday.

I was irate about this because, well, just because. Life was busy. Crazy busy. Tristan was still playing for the Seattle Stars. After he'd predicted he might only play another year or two after his knee injury, he was stronger than ever. At thirty-four years old, he definitely had more years of play in him now. The Stars had regrouped after the team had been shuffled with players getting traded and injuries sidelining others. The core of the Brit Boys was still holding though.

In the two years since that rainy night when we'd finally both faced the fact that we loved each other, much had changed while much remained the same. I'd actually taken over the very position Tristan had temporarily covered at the hospital during his break from soccer while he recovered from his injury. He was still declaring he'd be back to medicine, but I figured that was his retirement plan. I ran the research clinic at the hospital and took Lily to work with me where we had an on-site daycare.

Tristan had finally given up his completely pointless apartment about six months after that rainy night. We'd sold my duplex a year later and purchased a charming house in the same neighborhood where Liam and Olivia lived. I could walk down the street to see my bestie if I wanted, and I often did.

Oh, and we'd had Lily. I still couldn't get over it, but she'd been a surprise. I'd been on the pill for so long, I didn't think much about it. I'd had a nasty flu and completely forgotten to take the pill for a few days. I'd so thoroughly forgotten it, I didn't even think about it when I felt better. Until I got pregnant.

I looked over at Lily. She had Tristan's black curls and hazel eyes. She appeared to have been cursed with my personality—she was bold and reckless sometimes and generally a tornado in our house. My heart squeezed tightly when I glanced to Tristan.

He winked at me with a shrug. "Sorry luv. I totally forgot, and it wasn't on the list."

I shrugged. "I'm already over it."

He stood from the table and carted his now empty plate to the dishwasher, returning to fetch mine. I'd discovered he was a sublime cook. In the early months of our relationship, we were too busy screwing every chance we got for me to notice much of anything else. He'd gone so far above and beyond his initial promise to give me an orgasm, I could hardly remember it had ever been a problem for me.

He closed the dishwasher and paused behind my chair, sliding his hands down my arms and dipping his head to drop kisses along my neck. Shivers rolled through me.

"Why don't you drop Lily off and come

back home?" he murmured, the feel of his lips moving against my skin making my channel clench.

That's all it took, and my panties were wet. This man had ruined so many pairs of underwear at this point it was a joke. I angled my head, catching his eyes.

Oh God. His gaze was hot and dark. There was no question I'd be hurrying to drop Lily off and turning right back around.

***

TRISTAN

I watched Daisy hurry up the walkway toward me. I was waiting on the side porch of our home. It had only been maybe twenty minutes since she'd left to drop Lily off, and as far as my body was concerned, it felt like forever. As usual, she wore one of her tidy, barely professional outfits. Fuck me. I was quite certain I'd never get tired of the sight of her in one of her fitted skirts and blouses. I'd torn plenty of buttons off and intended to do just that right now. As soon as she cleared the top step, I caught her hand and reeled her to me.

Her lush bottom felt perfect in my palm.

I actually had somewhere to be, so I wasted no time. I spun us through the screen door. In a few stumbling steps, we were by the kitchen counter. I lifted her up, expecting to find her panties wet.

Instead of silk, I dragged my fingers through her bare, wet folds.

"You forgot something," I murmured against her lips.

She giggled and then moaned when I sank a finger into her. "No I didn't. They were a mess, so I took them off."

"We have five minutes."

"Well then, you'd best get to it."

Roughly fifteen minutes later—because we weren't very good at quickies—I dropped my head into her shoulder thinking for the thousandth time that I was exactly where I needed to be. With the scent of Daisy surrounding me and all of her close to me, my heart felt so full it was hard to believe I'd ever worried about relationships being messy. With Daisy, I'd take the mess all day, every day for the rest of my life.

Thank you for reading Play Me - I hope you loved Tristan & Daisy's story!

For more steamy romance, Jana & Finn's story is up next in Naughty Wish. Jana lands in Finn's police cruiser after a fender bender. Hijinks ensue, the holidays are right around the corner, and handcuffs might be involved! "If hearts could actually melt and pages catch fire, then they would with this story!" Don't miss Finn's story!

Keep reading for a sneak peek!

Be sure to sign up for my newsletter for the latest news, teasers & more! Click here to sign up: http://jhcroixauthor.com/subscribe/

Jana

My car lurched forward with a loud crunch. I'd been about to take a sip of coffee, only to have it spill all over my blouse. "Dammit!" I muttered to no one. I'd been inching along in Seattle's morning rush hour traffic and just gotten thumped in the bumper by the car behind me. On top of wondering how bad off my bumper was, I had coffee all over me.

"Great, just great. Exactly how I want to start my day."

I had a habit of talking to myself, especially when I was annoyed. I was in the far right lane—thank God—and slowly inched over to the side of the busy freeway. Snagging a napkin, I wiped the coffee splashed on my hand and dabbed at my blouse. Just my luck to be wearing a white blouse today. Climbing out, I smoothed my skirt, my eyes catching on the lovely new coffee stain on the side. I watched as the car that had run into me nearly clipped another bumper as the man driving it pulled over onto the shoulder.

He climbed out, slamming the door behind him, and stalking over to me where I waited by the guardrail. "Don't even try to tell me this was my fault," he said with a glare.

He wore—I kid you not—a bright yellow, shiny tracksuit.

"How the hell is this my fault?" I asked, throwing a glare right back at him.

"You stopped too fast," he declared, smoothing his hand over his slick, dark hair and crossing his arms.

Oh fuck that. I was not taking the blame for this. "There's a rule. If you hit the person in front of you, you were too close. There's no way that was my fault," I countered.

Tracksuit rolled his eyes. He was so cocky, he took my annoyance to the next level.

"Fine. Let's call the cops," he retorted with a smirk.

"Fine, let's."

I whipped my phone out and tapped out 9-1-1. I quickly reported our fender bender and then slipped my phone back in my purse before crossing my arms and leaning against my car.

"We'll just wait."

Tracksuit rolled his eyes again and leaned against his car. A few minutes later, I could see the lights of a police car approaching through the traffic. The police vehicle pulled over behind our cars. Within seconds, the police officer was climbing out, at which point Tracksuit decided to announce again that I'd been going too slow.

"Officer, she was also looking down at her phone," he added.

My cheeks got hot, and I pushed my hips off of my car, spinning to glare at him. "I was *not* looking at my phone you asshole!"

It was at this opportune moment our friendly cop arrived beside us, glancing down at me. I looked up at him and my breath caught in my throat. Oh. My. Wow. I loved a man in uniform. All by itself, a uniform was hot. Throw in this police officer's dark brown hair, deep blue eyes and a face to make me melt, well, I kinda melted a little right there.

He had sculpted cheekbones, a strong nose, a square jaw, and a sexy shadow of stubble. And his mouth, oh my God, his mouth. He had full, lush lips and a dimple in his chin.

Really, where the hell did he come from? They shouldn't make cops like him. It was dangerous. I would do anything he said right now. In fact, he could cuff me and take me away if he wanted.

I stayed quiet. I'd like to say I was strategically quiet, but I was actually speechless. That gave Tracksuit an opening.

"Not my fault. She was looking at her phone and slammed on her brakes," he announced.

Sexy cop eyed him for a moment and then looked to me. Oh this was just all kinds of bullshit. I got hot inside, probably a combination of the fact I was melting inside over sexy cop and angry with Tracksuit.

I glared at Tracksuit, temporarily forgetting about sexy cop. "I was *not* staring at my phone, and I did *not* slam on my brakes. I slowed down because I had to. In case you didn't notice..." I paused and gestured to the bumper to bumper traffic crawling along the crowded freeway "...it's rush hour."

I huffed and brushed my hair off my shoulder. Sexy cop glanced between us.

"Well this should be easy enough to resolve. You mind letting me check your phone?" he asked.

"Huh?" was my brilliant response.

"If I can confirm your phone wasn't in use, then it's easy."

There were laws about not using 'hand-held devices' when driving, but I hadn't been using my phone so there was nothing to see. I handed it over without even thinking. Small problem though. As soon as I handed it to him, I realized he would see my screensaver, which was a picture of a penis. That's right. A penis. It was a joke. A friend had a bache-lorette party and all the baked goods were naughty. My screensaver had a picture of a penis cake. It was so lifelike, I'd been unable to resist the urge to photograph it and proudly saved it to my phone. It made me laugh every time I looked at it. Great way to stay cheery.

I watched his eyes land on the screen and flick back to me. My cheeks heated. His gor-geous mouth curled at the corner, just the tiniest bit, and I couldn't help but grin.

His gorgeous blue eyes glinted with mirth, but he didn't laugh. He finally spoke. "You need to unlock it for me."

I almost forgot to mention sexy cop had a British accent. Where in God's name did a British cop come from in Seattle? I didn't know, but he could talk to me all day. It was that awesome. I was downright flustered at this point, my body humming so hard I was almost loopy. I might've been embarrassed he'd seen the penis cake, but the little hint of a grin was enough to set me on fire inside. I quickly took my phone back and tapped out my password.

"There. Look at whatever you need," I announced, remembering to throw a glare in Tracksuit's direction.

Tracksuit simply rolled his eyes and crossed his arms again.

Sexy cop caught my eyes. "I can look at anything?"

The corner of his mouth hitched up again. My cheeks got even hotter. I shrugged and adjusted my purse on my shoulder. "I have nothing to hide."

He arched a brow and glanced down at my phone screen. "I'd say not," he murmured.

I twirled a lock of my hair around my finger, watching as he pulled up my texts and calls before handing my phone back to me. His eyes held the barest hint of a gleam, flicking down to my screen again as the cake penis reappeared when he closed out the list of calls.

"All I needed to see were your calls, texts and activity log. Entirely unnecessary to see anything else," he said.

The sound of his voice sent a shiver up my spine and heat unfurling in a wave through my body. All I could manage was a nod.

Sexy cop glanced from Tracksuit to me. "There's no evidence her phone was in use. It's heavy traffic, and you were behind her, likely following too closely."

He paused and Tracksuit jumped in.

"That's bullshit. I know…"

I temporarily forgot my speechless state. Aside from being an obnoxious jerk, Tracksuit sadly reminded me of my last boss. He had the same cocky attitude. My last boss had pretty much ruined my life. Mistake number one: never date your boss. That itself was bad enough, but the worst part was I didn't actually know he was married. How I missed that massively relevant detail, I didn't know. Anyway, in short, it blew up my life, and Tracksuit reminded me of him.

"You fucking asshole! It's *not* bullshit. I wasn't on my phone. You bumped into me. Shut up and deal…"

Sexy cop put his hand on my arm, effectively ending my tirade. Just the feel of his hand on me made me hot all over and snapped me out of my focus on Tracksuit. I glanced over at him. The moment I met his eyes, I discovered I could happily stare at him all day.

"Yes?"

"Entirely unnecessary to argue," he said, that slightly haughty tone of his sending my belly in a spinning flip.

I scrambled my thoughts together when he arched a brow, making me quite aware I was staring dumbly at him. "Right. So what now? My bumper's dented," I said, pointing to the crushed corner of said bumper. I drove a small, bright blue hatchback that had honestly seen better days, but I was rather attached to it. My little car had seen me through some rough years.

Sexy cop's eyes glanced to my car and back to me. "I'll write a citation, and you'll follow up with your insurance company," he said simply.

All very logical. I nodded, and he let go of my arm. Tracksuit seemed to have decided it wasn't worth arguing and leaned against his car, staring into traffic.

Sexy cop stepped away and responded to the voice crackling in the radio mounted on his shoulder. In short order, he wrote up a citation while I exchanged insurance information with Tracksuit.

Tracksuit drove away, still throwing glares

at me. I ignored him and rounded the back of my car, only then noticing I had a flat tire.

I spun back and almost collided with sexy cop. My mouth went dry when I met his gaze. Sweet hell. He was so damn hot, it wasn't fair.

Somehow I managed to form words. "I have a flat tire."

It was a damn miracle I didn't melt into a puddle at his feet.

Available Now!

Naughty Wish

Go here to sign up for information on new releases: http://jhcroixauthor.com/subscribe/

For a sneak peek of my latest series, check out Burn For Me - a second chance romance for the ages. Sexy firefighters? Check. Rugged men? Check. Wrapped up together? Check. Brave the fire in these hot, small-town romances.

AMELIA

I shoved through the door into the bar, coming to a quick stop as my eyes adjusted to the light. I brushed a wet lock of hair off of my cheek and threaded through the tables to the bar at the back. Once I slipped onto a stool, the bartender spun to face me. He was a jolly looking man with round blue eyes.

"I'm Tank. You look like you could use a drink," he announced, his wide smile softening his observation.

"A beer will do," I replied.

"House draft okay?" he asked.

At my nod, he spun around. Within seconds, he'd handed me my beer and silently offered a clean towel. Though it was tiny, seeing as it was a bar towel, I quickly scrubbed it over my dripping wet hair and face before handing it back to him. I settled in to try to forget my shitty day.

A bit later, I drained my beer and glanced around the bar, savoring the anonymity of being in a crowded bar in Anchorage, Alaska where no one knew me. I was tucked in the corner by the wall, pleased to have a nice view of the crowd and yet go unnoticed by just about everyone there. Tank caught my eyes again, a question held in them. I nodded and held my empty pint glass aloft. He nodded in return while he mixed a drink for someone and pulled another pint for me with his free hand. The extent of my conversation with anyone this evening had been limited to Tank's earlier introduction.

If he thought anything awry with the fact I was wearing a wedding dress splashed with mud, he didn't show it. Neither did anyone around me. Anchorage was just large enough of a city people left you alone if you appeared to want to be left as such. That said, people were friendly too. Alaska, despite its sprawling geography, kept its residents close, all bound by the knowledge they lived on the edge of the wild and had the strength and guts for such a life.

I took a drag on what was my third beer and wondered if perhaps I should slow down. I was definitely tipsy and on my way to drunk. I fingered the cream silk of my wedding dress. Or maybe I needed to consider it my not-wedding dress. I'd been all dressed and ready to go when I'd failed in my battle against the knot of tension balled like a vise around my heart. I swallowed against the rush of emotion that rose inside as my eyes traveled down the fitted bodice of my dress and bounced to the muddy splotches all over its swirling skirt. Oh yeah. I hadn't simply ditched my groom-to-be just before we got to the altar, I'd bolted in the rain. Another swallow of beer, followed with a slow sigh. What stung the most—all I felt was relief. Not regret, not second thoughts. Just pure relief.

I'd walked across the hallway at the back of the church and barged into Earl's dressing room. There he'd stood, tall and handsome with his dark blonde hair and brown eyes. It was what I never saw in his eyes when he looked at me that pushed me to tell him I couldn't marry him. When Earl looked at me, I saw a kind regard, a humored attempt to appreciate me for who I was. Yet, there was never anything close to the hot fire I'd known once upon a time with someone else. I'd apologized, but I'd also been flat pissed with him for trying to trick himself and me into thinking he really loved me.

A dash into the late afternoon rain on a cool summer day in Alaska had felt cleansing. Until I got chilled and finally ducked into this bar. I didn't even know what it was called. I suddenly recalled I didn't have a penny on me. It wasn't like I'd been carrying a purse for my aborted walk up the aisle. Oh well, oh hell. I caught sight of my reflection in the mirror behind the bar and bit back a sigh. My amber hair was a damp, tangled mess.

I didn't think much about how I looked. To be honest, it was more that I tried not to. I was as tall as most men. I ran my own construction business to boot. I tried to never let it show, but when it came to my femininity, seeds of doubt were planted firmly inside. It didn't help that all but one man treated me pretty much like a man, Earl included.

I gave my head a hard shake and glanced around the bar again, scanning the collection of people. Businessmen rubbed elbows with fishermen here. Sports reigned supreme on the televisions screens mounted at various points in the bar, and a few pool tables were clustered in the corner. That's what I'd do. I loved pool and was pretty damn good at it.

A few minutes later, I was paired up in a game with three other guys. They'd thrown a few looks askance at my wedding dress and seemed amused at playing with me. Tipsy and deep into my *don't give a damn* mode, I set out to beat them.

Roughly an hour later, I grinned as my last ball rolled neatly into a pocket corner. "Well, boys," I said, glancing among them.

The boys in question had been drinking and gotten steadily more sullen as we played. One of them, a hulking sort with dark eyes and hair, glared at me. They'd bet on this game after the first two, and I was due five dollars each from them.

Mr. Hulk, as I'd come to call him in my head, stepped close to me, too close for comfort. "No fiver from any of us. You got that?"

I was just drunk enough not to care. I stretched up to my full five foot eleven inches. He might have more bulk than me, but I was a hair taller. "Ah, I see. You only like to bet if you're gonna win? What an ass," I said, my lips curling in a sneer.

I was stretched too thin emotionally with

white hot anger, a simmering anger I'd kept buried for the entirety of the two years I'd wasted on Earl, and a tad too drunk to be reasonable right now. When the jerk stepped closer and put his finger on my chest, I didn't even think. I punched him, right in the nose.

"You fuckin' bitch!" he shouted as he swiped his sleeve across his face, smearing the blood from his nose on his cheek.

He hauled off and punched me back, his fist bouncing under my eye. He had enough heft to send me tumbling to the floor, an inglorious heap of muddied silk spilling around me. I was just tipsy enough not to care that my face was throbbing. Without the mud, minus the dingy hardwood floor under me and definitely minus the crowd now gathered around, I considered the way the silk of my dress spilled in a near perfect circle would have made a great wedding photo—one of those candid shots people would love.

In a flash, Tank was there, shoving the guy who'd punched me away. Voices above me collided with each other.

"Dude, she hit me first!"

"Self defense..."

"Yeah, but she's a girl..."

"She's a fuckin' giant, and she can hit. She's no girl!"

I closed my eyes and wished I could crawl into a hole. The buzz that had kept me afloat this afternoon and evening dissolved into mortification. The jerk was right. I was a giant and no one would ever look at me and think girly thoughts.

"Amelia?"

My heartbeat came to a screeching stop and then jumpstarted with a hard kick. I'd know that voice anywhere. Through the jumble around me with Tank leaning over to ask if I was okay, that voice rang like a loud bell inside. One man. Only one man had ever looked at me with heat in his eyes, heat so hot it singed me. That man spoke my name now. I didn't have to open my eyes to know. I did anyway. Because I couldn't bear not to see him.

Cade Masters stood at the edge of the circle gathered around me, another man in a bar crowded with men. Shaggy dark brown hair, green eyes, and a body of raw muscle stood before me. My heart felt as if it had been split open. I'd loved Cade in that wild headlong way that only youth allowed. No more than seven years had passed since I'd seen him, but it felt like forever. Cade had broken my heart and walked out of my life when I was twenty-two. He hadn't just broken my heart, he'd betrayed me.

Anger flashed hot and high inside, yet I couldn't look away. My eyes ate Cade up. He wore faded jeans, the fabric so worn it hugged his muscled legs like a caress, and a denim jacket over a black t-shirt. He had something of an outdoorsy, biker vibe. Once upon a time, he'd taken me on long rides on his motorcycle through the nearly empty highways in Alaska surrounding our hometown. He stepped through the crowd and knelt at my side, his green gaze coasting over me. "You okay?" he asked.

I nodded without really thinking about it. He lifted a hand and ran the backs of his fingers along my cheekbone. Oh right, some guy had just punched me in the face. Cade's presence had wiped my mind clean of everything else. With barely a brush of his touch, my heart fluttered and heat tightened inside.

"You sure?"

I swallowed, suddenly aware of my throbbing cheek. My entire day flashed through my mind. A gloriously shitty day. I fought against the tears, but they welled up, unbidden and beyond my control. One tear rolled down my cheek and then another and another. Of all the times and places to encounter the one and only man who still held a piece of my heart, this had to be the absolute worst.

Cade's eyes never left mine. Something flickered deep in the depths of them, but I didn't know how to interpret it. Without a word, he slipped his arm around my waist and lifted me up, bundling me into his arms as if it was the most normal thing in the world to do. "Let's get you out of here," he said and started to stride away.

Tank caught him by the arm, and Cade glanced to him. "Yeah?"

"Just making sure she's okay," Tank replied.

All I could do was nod. I was so totally *not* okay, but I was okay in the sense Tank was asking.

Tank's warm gaze held mine, this bartender who barely knew me, but had somehow known I'd had a bad day and just needed to be left in peace while I had a few beers. I should've stayed put in my seat at the bar. My raw emotions and crazy day, all of my own making if I was being honest with myself, had gotten me into this mess.

"You want the police involved?" Tank asked.

I shook my head and finally found my

voice. "No. Let's call it even. I punched him, he punched me."

"You know this guy?" Tank asked next, nodding to Cade.

"Uh huh. It's okay. He's an old friend of my family's. No need to worry," I managed. On its face, my explanation was true. Cade and I had grown up together in Willow Brook, Alaska. Our families had known each other for years. Yet, my explanation left out so much of what Cade meant to me, it was almost laughable.

Tank released his grip on Cade's arm and let us be. Cade was quiet as he strode through the bar, the crowd parting around him. I could only imagine how we looked— me in my dirty not-wedding dress and him giving off his usual *back the hell off* vibes. It was a shock to see him for the first time in years and even more of a shock to be held in his arms. I felt at home in his strong embrace. He held me easily. He always had. I loved that about him. Cade was a good four inches taller than me at six foot three inches and had never cared about how tall I was. He pushed through the door of the bar, stepping out into the late evening. The rain had stopped at some point during the long hours I'd been hiding in the bar.

He paused once they were outside on the sidewalk and glanced down, his gaze catching mine. "Why are you wearing a wedding dress?"

Available Now!

Burn For Me

Go here to sign up for information on new releases: http://jhcroixauthor.com/subscribe/

Thank you for reading Play Me! I hope you enjoyed the story. If so, you can help other readers find my books in a variety of ways.

1) Write a review!
2) Sign up for my newsletter, so you can receive information about upcoming new releases & receive a FREE copy of one of my books: http://jhcroixauthor.com/subscribe/
3) Like and follow my Amazon Author page at https://amazon.com/author/jhcroix
4) Follow me on Bookbub at https://www.bookbub.com/authors/j-h-croix

5) Follow me on Instagram https://www.
instagram.com/jhcroix/
6) Like my Facebook page at https://www.
facebook.com/jhcroix

———

Brit Boys Sports Romance
The Play
Big Win
Out Of Bounds
Play Me
Naughty Wish
Swoon Series
This Crazy Love
Wait For Me
Break My Fall
Truly Madly Mine
Into The Fire Series
Burn For Me
Slow Burn
Burn So Bad
Hot Mess
Burn So Good
Sweet Fire
Play With Fire
Melt With You
Burn For You
Crash & Burn

Diamond Creek Alaska Novels

When Love Comes

Follow Love

Love Unbroken

Love Untamed

Tumble Into Love

Christmas Nights

Last Frontier Lodge Novels

Christmas on the Last Frontier

Love at Last

Just This Once

Falling Fast

Stay With Me

When We Fall

Hold Me Close

Crazy For You

Just Us

Catamount Lion Shifters

Protected Mate

Chosen Mate

Fated Mate

Destined Mate

A Catamount Christmas

The Lion Within

Lion Lost & Found

ACKNOWLEDGMENTS

This one goes out to my mom. I finished this book up right when she was busy reminding me life is what you make of it. For her, it's all about actions, not words. To one of the strongest women I know - cheers Mom! Gracious thanks to Yoly Cortez from Cormar Covers for creating an entire series of amazing covers. My editor held my feet to the fire on this one and made sure Tristan was all the man he was supposed to be. Special thanks to my proofreader angels - Beth P., Terri E., Janine & now Terri D. You never let my books go out without making sure they're just so. Always...my readers. Thank you from the bottom of my heart for cheering my books on!

xoxo
J.H. Croix

ABOUT THE AUTHOR

USA Today Bestselling Author J. H. Croix lives in a small town in the historical farmlands of Maine with her husband and two spoiled dogs. Croix writes steamy contemporary romance with sassy independent women and rugged alpha men who aren't afraid to show some emotion. Her love for quirky small-towns and the characters that inhabit them shines through in her writing. Take a walk on the wild side of romance with her bestselling novels!

Places you can find me:
jhcroixauthor.com
jhcroix@jhcroix.com